I ONLY KILLED HIM ONCE

Also available from Adam Christopher and Titan Books

THE SPIDER WARS
The Burning Dark
The Machine Awakes
The Dead Stars (January 2019)

THE LA TRILOGY
Made to Kill
Killing is My Business
I Only Killed Him Once

ELEMENTARY
The Ghost Line
Blood and Ink

ADAM CHRISTOPHER

I ONLY KILLED HIM ONCE

THE LA TRILOGY — BOOK III

TITANBOOKS

I Only Killed Him Once
Print edition ISBN: 9781783296897
E-book edition ISBN: 9781783296903

Published by Titan Books
A division of Titan Publishing Group Ltd
144 Southwark Street, London SE1 0UP

First edition: July 2018
2 4 6 8 10 9 7 5 3 1

This is a work of fiction. Names, characters, places, and incidents either are the product of the author's imagination or are used fictitiously, and any resemblance to actual persons, living or dead, business establishments, events, or locales is entirely coincidental. The publisher does not have any control over and does not assume any responsibility for author or third-party websites or their content.

A CIP catalogue record for this title is available from the British Library.

Printed and bound in Great Britain by CPI Group Ltd.

Did you enjoy this book? We love to hear from our readers. Please email us at: readerfeedback@titanemail.com, or write to us at the above address.

To receive advance information, news, competitions, and exclusive offers online, please sign up for the Titan newsletter on our website.
www.titanbooks.com

For Sandra

*As to the ending or denouement not being a surprise—
what ending is?*

—*Raymond Chandler, 1954*

I ONLY KILLED HIM ONCE

1

They say you should never start with the weather, but look, it was a dark and stormy night and I don't care who knows it.

I was sitting in my car and my car was sitting in a parking lot, and me and the car and the parking lot were all gathered together for this little meeting in Hollywood, California. It was raining, and when I say the rain was heavy, think pounding waves and crashing seas and a full couple of inches of water being buffeted into an impressive surf all across the flat tarmacadam that surrounded my car and all the other cars that were lined up outside the restaurant.

There had been a warning about the weather. Apparently it was on the television. Ada had told me about it. The day was one for the books, the television said. I didn't know if that was true. I didn't remember the weather earlier than six this morning. It had been raining then too and the rain had only gotten worse.

I didn't much like the rain but Ada said it was good for business, and as I sat in the car and listened to the tempest I had to say I agreed with her. People move fast in the rain— they move fast and they keep their heads down and they don't have much on their minds except getting from point A to point B without getting their ankles wet. Whatever else was going on around them could take a hike, at least while the heavens were open and the angels were rinsing their togas.

I had put the radio on when I had set off out of the garage underneath the building on the corner of Cahuenga Pass and Hollywood Boulevard where I had my office and no sooner had I taken a right turn when the deejay told me to turn back around and park my car and settle in for an evening of hot cocoa and cold show tunes from decades past.

I ignored his advice and I kept driving. I had a job to do and tonight was the best night to do it and come hell or high water I was going to get it done.

High water it was. The drive across town had been long and arduous and the capabilities of my Buick's windshield wipers were now sorely in question.

The restaurant was a diner called—according to the huge construction of multicolored neon letters that floated in the black, wet air some distance over the roof of the establishment—Pepi's. The sign flashed and strobed and buzzed in the rain, the electrified gases within those tubes producing the illusion of a moving arrow pointing down into the parking lot. The sign also featured a series of concentric ellipses expanding outward around what looked like a representation of the owner's signature. The sign was so bright it lit up the rain around it, making a whole patch of night air glow, surrounding itself with a fuzzy halo.

I liked the sign. It wasn't just a functional piece of street furniture. The sign was a work of art by someone who clearly loved their job. I thought it was great and it was actually pretty welcoming, particularly with the greater Los Angeles area apparently engulfed in a cyclone, although the way the sign was buffeted in the wind was less than comforting. The whole thing was stuck on a pole so thin and insubstantial I was of half a mind to move my car in case it came down on top of it.

I didn't. The wind blew up and then it calmed down into a kind of rhythm and the sign wobbled but stayed up. As I sat in my car watching the restaurant, I found myself watching the sign almost as often. I wondered if I could have a sign like that for my office. Something smaller, of course, but I had some wall space available. Maybe I'd need to move the filing cabinet. Sure, it would be a strange thing, but then the only person who was ever in the office was me because it wasn't a real office, not really. It was a hangover, nothing more, from a previous life when the Electromatic Detective Agency had been exactly that and nothing more and I was an electronic private eye and nothing more.

Now I was an electronic private killer, and nobody came to the office, but I still thought a neon sign would be a nice thing to have. Call it an art installation. It was 1965, after all. Maybe Ada would like it too.

Then I focused my optics on the job at hand. Things were

starting to happen in the diner, and I hadn't come out in a flood just to get my tires wet while I admired a street sign.

Pepi's was a long, low building made out of curved aluminum siding with a mirrorlike finish, the metal and the water that flowed down it reflecting the multicolored wonder of the neon sign. The walls were ridged like a trailer, although as far as I could tell the building wasn't built to move. It had a red roof that wasn't quite flat and big red double doors and windows all around three sides that were also big and also framed in red. There was an awning stretched out along the whole front of the joint. The awning bounced in the wind and the rain sprayed back up into the air in a mist so thick that when the neon sign flashed red it looked like Pepi had set his grill too high and lit the place afire.

I checked my watch and then I checked my internal chronometer just to be sure. They both told me it was coming up on nine in the evening. But despite the hour and despite the weather the place was doing steady business. From my position behind the wheel I could see into Pepi's pretty well, the rain so heavy it ran what was effectively a single, solid sheet down the windshield, which did nothing to my view except to make it ripple a little.

Inside the restaurant were five occupied tables, three by the front windows and two farther back, and I could see three waitresses moving around in red-and-white uniforms. There was a young man in white busy behind the main counter and behind him there was another man working the grill. My view was so good I could even read the menus that hung over the counter if I zoomed in a little.

The three tables at the front were booths. The one

nearest the restaurant's doors was occupied by a trio, two teenage girls dressed like cheerleaders and one teenage boy dressed like a jock. He had red hair and one of the girls was a blonde and the other a brunette and they laughed and drank their milkshakes and all was right with the world.

In the next booth along sat an older couple. She was blond and wore a dress almost the same color as her hair. What hair the man had left was mouse brown and he wore glasses and they were both more interested in their chicken salads than each other.

The next booth was empty. The one after that had, until a minute ago, been home to just one man. He was wearing a black suit with a black tie and white shirt. I'd gotten into position after he had come in, but I assumed the long, wet black coat hanging on the chromium hook by the doors was his, as was the black hat with black band that sat on the table in front of him. He'd been there awhile, and despite the persuasive nature of Pepi's servers, he had yet to order anything and any conversation he'd had with the staff had been short and to the point, but on a night like this Pepi and his staff were clearly pleased enough to have some company so the black-suited customer had been permitted to stay without giving the place his custom.

A couple of times the man in the booth had looked out of the windows and he had looked straight at me, but I knew I was safe. The lights inside the restaurant were bright and white, and while the parking lot was lit in moving reds and yellows and blues by Pepi's magical neon sign, that helped me a great deal, given I was sitting inside a dark car behind a windshield slick with water. I didn't need to breathe, on account of the fact that I was a wonder of electronic wizardry and mechanical genius, so none of the windows were in any danger of fogging up. If the guy at the booth had been looking at me all he would have seen was the shape of a largish car like all the other largish cars in the lot and the mirrored shapes of the big neon letters reflected back at him from the windshield.

The man had piloted his booth solo for a good half hour when he was joined by someone, although it wasn't that someone that had got my attention. It was the reaction of everyone else in the restaurant when he walked through the doors.

He'd driven into the lot in a small, low car with a sharp front and big wheels and no backseat to speak of. He'd parked close to the main doors, not in a slot allocated for vehicles but at an angle that suggested he either owned the place or thought he did. That left him only a few yards to swim to the entrance, which he did with a beige trench coat pulled up and over his head. That coat made it onto the chromium hook alongside the black coat, and that's when people started getting excited.

It was the teenagers first. The two girls had their backs toward the door and their eyes locked on the jock, and when I zoomed in I could see the disappointed confusion scudding across their faces as the jock's eyes went up, followed by his chin, followed by his athletic behind as he lifted himself up, just a few inches, to get a better look at the newcomer. Of the two girls, the blond one turned first, and then almost as quickly her hand shot out and she grabbed the shoulder of her friend and pulled her around too. Their milkshake nearly went over but the trio had suddenly lost all interest in it.

The object of their attention walked across the length of the diner, from my right to my left. As he passed the booth of kids I zoomed out, my optics skipping as they tried to get a focus on the newcomer's jacket. It was plaid, yellow and white and black, and there was some red too and maybe some green and it played merry havoc with my vertical hold. No wonder the kids were mesmerized by him. The CIA could use the pattern of the fabric to brainwash a foreign agent.

There was something about him that I couldn't quite put a finger on. As I watched I reached for the yellow legal pad on the passenger seat next to me and with a mechanical pencil I made a note or two.

Memory like mine, I found it paid to take notes.

The older lady in the middle booth saw the newcomer from the corner of her eye and those eyes followed him as he made his way across the restaurant. While the jock stared and the cheerleaders whispered to each other, the woman just smiled, and she looked happy and relaxed and she looked like she was remembering an old story from long ago and maybe she was imagining she wasn't in Pepi's diner on a wet and wild night with a man, perhaps her husband, who continued to work at his salad and didn't look up.

The newcomer reached the man in the booth. He gave a nod and slid in sideways. His jaw was as square as cut glass and when he spoke about a million white teeth did their best to outshine what I supposed he thought was a sport coat. He smiled as he talked and when the waitress came over he smiled some more. The waitress took an awful long time with the order, and when she went back to the diner's counter her first port of call wasn't the kitchen but the other servers, who were all standing and looking and smiling with shoulders hunched, heads ducked down, their bodies together in a way that was not entirely dissimilar to the reaction of the cheerleaders at the first booth. The older guy with the glasses was missing out. I wondered if I should walk up to the glass and knock, tell him to stop fussing with his lettuce and mayo and take a good look behind him.

As for me, who the newcomer was I didn't know and I didn't care. But the other guy in the booth, the man with the black hair and expression as friendly as the weather, I knew three things about.

First, that his name was Touch Daley.

Second, that he was a G-man.

Third, that I was going to kill him.

2

Touch Daley and his guest stayed at the table in the window a real long time. As they talked, Daley's expression went through a whole range of emotions from depressingly gloomy to vaguely disgusted. I couldn't blame him, sitting opposite a jacket like the one his guest was wearing. I also didn't blame him for not eating or drinking. While his companion had a burger with fries and a Coke in a glass bottle with a long, striped straw, Daley settled in with a big mug of hot coffee and a stainless steel carafe of the stuff at his elbow.

He didn't touch either of them.

I couldn't hear what they were saying but then again I didn't need to. Maybe if I really tried hard I could make a fair stab at lip reading but, again, why bother. I had no idea who the guy in the jacket was and it didn't matter. I was here for Mr. Daley. All I had to do was sit and wait, and I could do both quite nicely from the comfort and dryness of my car.

Not that I needed much comfort. I was six feet and ten inches of bronzed titanium alloy made to a secret government recipe. Underneath that alloy was a lot of magical gadgetry, state of the art you'd call it, although I had no idea what that meant. Because what was inside me was not art but pure science, the end product of years of research and development and experimentation.

I guess any sufficiently advanced technology is indistinguishable from art. I pondered that sentiment for a while and I decided I liked it. I wondered if it was something that Professor Thornton used to say. It sounded like it was.

As for me being the end product, I really was. I was the last robot off the production line, the date of my activation the official closing date of the federal robot program: March 26, 1959. I was the most advanced machine the human race had ever built, and I was the only one of my kind. I guess a lot of money had been spent already, and if there was one thing government pencil-pushers didn't like much at all it was spending a lot of money. They needed a return on their investment and I guess the Professor had promised them the world. So they allowed him to keep the doors of Thornton Industrial Electronics and Research open just a little bit longer. Figuratively speaking. That operation in Pasadena was just one of several sites the Department of Robot Labor had authorized Thornton to run with federal funding, and he had others that ran just fine without their help, including his own personal lab somewhere near a beach in Southern California that probably also counted as state of the art.

The laboratory. Not the beach.

And then that last little project was done and that project was me, the last robot in the world, the sole survivor of a decade and a half of a robot workforce that had come and gone. Thornton Industrial Electronics and Research was mothballed along with everything else. Including the good professor.

That much I knew. It was on my permanent store, a repository of useful information that I needed to operate in a world of humans. I knew what cows were and how airplanes worked and the best recipe for a gimlet (half gin and half Rose's lime juice and nothing else and don't let anyone tell you otherwise).

And that was just fine. It was my other memory that was an issue. Professor Thornton, genius he truly was, built a compact reel-to-reel memory tape that sat in my not insubstantial chest cavity. The micro tape in question had the capacity to record everything I did during a single day. But twenty-four hours, and that was it. When my time was up, the tape came out and I was given a clean one and the world was born anew.

A fact that made the yellow legal pad currently sitting on my knee an interesting, not to say vital, development.

It had been on the passenger seat of the car when I had gotten into it back at the garage. It was about half done, the pages neatly torn off the top but leaving a ragged ribbon next to the glue. The top few pages on the remaining pad had the impression of writing on them, and if I held the pad up and tilted it to the light I could see some of it, even read a little. Cycling through filters on my optics made a little difference but not much, but what was legible wasn't anything I could understand, anyway. It was mostly single words, some circled—several times in a couple of cases—and I could make out a lot of question marks and even an arrow or two connecting short statements. What the notes were about was a mystery.

But I did know one thing. The notes were mine. I didn't remember making them but I knew my handwriting when I saw it. I must have left the notepad out in the open on the seat like that to get my attention the next day. Given how much of the pad was used it occurred to me that I had been doing it awhile.

If only I had written something a little clearer. *Ray's Little Book of Secrets* would have been more useful.

So I sat in the car and I kept the notepad on my knee and I switched my attention back to the diner. As I watched Touch Daley and his buddy I ignored the growing desire for a carafe of coffee of my own. I pondered getting a container to go, but that would mean getting wet and the coffee would steam up my windows, which would make surveillance more difficult than it was right now, so I let it slide. And besides, I wasn't entirely sure I wanted Touch Daley—or anyone else in the diner, for that matter—to see me. A robot walking into a restaurant in the middle of a storm and asking for coffee to go was something I could imagine people would tend to remember when asked, and in my line of work it was fairly important that people didn't remember me at all.

So I sat and I watched. Touch's coffee must have been getting cold. The guy in the jacket had finished his food and got a carafe of his own. That seemed like a waste but then it wasn't on my dime so what did I care.

Touch Daley. He had an interesting name. A nickname perhaps. Or perhaps not. This was Hollywood, after all. I didn't know what branch of the federal government he worked for but he looked like the kind of man who worked for a certain kind of agency, the ones that were full of a certain kind of man and had a certain kind of way of dressing them, all black hats and black coats and narrow ties. The kind of agency where smiling was forbidden, where the training program involved practicing an array of expressions from mildly annoyed to slightly angry.

At least, that's what came to mind when I watched him, and I didn't know why it did so I just put it down to another little gift from Professor Thornton. I was doing a lot of that today. It was an easy explanation and maybe a lazy one, but the truth was that in order to give me a mind and a personality all of my own, Thornton had used his own as a template. How that actually worked I didn't know because that information was locked away in a part of my permanent store that I didn't need to access, the area that was filled with raw program codes and machine algorithms that told my microswitches which way was up.

But having Thornton's template meant that I had a part of Thornton with me all the time and it meant that I enjoyed the smell of pipe tobacco and had opinions about baseball and the Fermi paradox. And maybe Thornton had watched too many cheap TV thrillers, ones filled with actors wrapped in black suits doing the best interpretation of men like Touch Daley.

Or maybe Thornton had dealt with his fair share of government agents in dark suits during his time at the lab. Given the nature of his work, that seemed a distinct likelihood—maybe he'd even dealt with Touch Daley. Because the name certainly rang a bell.

That was also something that happened sometimes. I called them fragments, and they usually rose up in my circuits like a slowly increasing voltage, giving me hunches or vague ideas. Less often they came as flashes that for a nanosecond took over all my sensory inputs and put me somewhere else, sometime else.

These fragments and flashes were an artifact, nothing more than electric dreams caused by my memory systems operating at the very edge of technology. The small tape in my chest was one of only a small number and they were all reused in rotation after being copied onto larger archive tapes. These big tapes were stored in a secret room hidden behind the office. But the erasure of the smaller, portable tapes was never perfect, and sometimes data got stuck in the cracks and sometimes I could read that data and I got ideas.

Or feelings. Like now. Because there was no flash and no vision but I had a feeling that I knew who Touch Daley was. But it didn't matter anyway. Not to the job. All I had to do was find Touch Daley and make sure he never had another cup of coffee after tonight.

So far I was halfway home.

But I wrote some notes anyway. As I wrote them I wondered where the rest of the pad was. I must have written a hundred pages and hidden them somewhere. And I knew that each and every day I would have made the same discovery and come to the same conclusions.

I looked up at the diner. The rain had eased and the diner

was empty now apart from Daley and the guy in the jacket and the man who had previously been running the grill. He was now standing behind the counter and watching his last two customers. He was dressed in an apron and garrison cap sharp enough for a parade at West Point and he had a neat little gray moustache. He must have been the legendary Pepi himself. The lips under that moustache of his were twisting this way and that and he had his arms folded and he sometimes checked his watch. He was clearly eager to shut up shop and get back home to punch out a few army drills.

My target didn't seem to notice. He was still talking and maybe his peripheral vision was being dazzled by the other guy's jacket. The other guy just grinned and jammed the last of his French fries into his mouth. He shook his head while he grinned. Something was amusing. Whatever Daley was selling, the guy in the jacket wasn't buying.

I think I liked him, whoever he was. Apart from the fact that he was making a short job long and I had to get back to the office by dawn.

But then some of that luck I had been thinking about knocked on my door and walked right in. Touch Daley stopped talking and he picked up his hat and adjusted the brim with two long fingers and then he put the hat on while the other guy sat there watching and chewing his fries and enjoying the show. Then Touch Daley stood up and left the table and his coffee carafe and his untouched coffee mug and he turned and headed to the door. Pepi didn't move from the counter but he watched him go. The other guy started to get busy with napkins and then he waved a hand to get Pepi's attention.

But my optics were on Touch Daley. He paused at the chromium hook to get his black coat and then he put it on and then he opened the doors and he tripped down the steps of the diner without any particular concern for the weather. I found myself putting the notepad back on the passenger seat and leaning forward over the wheel as I watched him.

But he didn't head for the parking lot. Instead he skirted the silver side of the diner and walked right past the window where my guy was giving Pepi another order. Then Touch Daley hit the street and he turned his back to me and he walked off into the night under the flashing colors of the neon sign. A moment later he had vanished into the hazy dark.

I was surprised he hadn't come by car. The diner wasn't far from anywhere, but the night was not a friendly one and I was of the opinion that people didn't walk anywhere in Los Angeles.

Showed what I knew.

But then again, he could have parked his car around the corner. The meeting hardly seemed a secret and my guy had parked his sportsmobile practically by the milkshake machine, but maybe Touch Daley was just following procedure. I glanced around the parking lot. There were still several cars around mine but none of them belonged to anybody in the diner, given that there was only Pepi and the other guy left and it seemed unlikely that Pepi kept a fleet of mid-priced sedans lined up outside his restaurant so he could look out over his automotive empire while he worked.

Touch Daley had either stashed his vehicle in a dark

and narrow alley or maybe he had a comrade waiting, accelerator gunning, headlights low, sitting tight until his boss came back and gave the order for blast off.

Or maybe the damp had got into my neutronic ignition line and was giving me funny ideas. I had a job to do and sitting in the rain in a parking lot was not the way to do it.

I started my car and I kept the headlights off as I eased back clear out of my slot and then I danced a leather-clad bronzed-titanium toe on the gas as I rolled the car as quietly as I could to the exit. Out of the glare of the neon the night opened up around me and looking right I saw a tall dark shape I knew was my target walking down the sidewalk, his back to me, the rain bouncing off his hat and his shoulders like he didn't have a care in the world.

He was about to have a care, all right.

It was late. The street was clear. As was the sidewalk. I knew this part of town well and I knew just the right kind of places nearby that would come in handy for a job like mine.

I turned left and turned the lights on and turned my speed up and the shape of Touch Daley loomed bigger in my windshield as I came in for my final approach.

Later I sat in the car awhile in the garage underneath my office. The rain had picked up again and I could hear the roar of it on the street outside even from down the garage ramp. There were still a few hours until dawn. I had some time left.

Time to do some thinking.

Maybe even time to do a little of that detective work I used to be good at in a previous life.

In point of fact I sat in the car long enough for the telephone at my elbow to ring twice. I knew who it was and I ignored it both times. It wasn't that Ada was worried. She might have been the boss, a computer the size of a good-sized room who ran the operation and got me to do the legwork, but despite my not insignificant limitations I was a big robot and I could look after myself and Ada knew that.

But she would also know that I was in the garage. She would be wondering what I was doing down there, sitting in my car with the engine off, listening to the rain, contemplating the night.

Contemplating the job.

I felt a condenser click. I felt a logic gate flip. I felt the voltage surge in a circuit or two.

The job.

I wasn't in the habit of laughing. In fact, I wasn't programmed for it. But there was something there, an itch at the back of my vanadium-lined vocalizer. There was a little flap behind the grille that formed my mouth and when it opened, the sound that came out was more like a truck with a desperate need for new brakes than anything you'd recognize as an expression of mirth.

The job.

Oh brother, the job.

I glanced down at the passenger seat. Sitting on it was a hat and it wasn't mine. It was smaller than my usual fedora. It was a trilby and it was black and it was wet and it had once belonged to the dearly departed Touch Daley.

I'd removed it from his head after the job and I had decided to keep it and I still didn't know why. It wasn't a souvenir. It couldn't be. Part of the reason why I was so good at my job is that as well as not remembering things I didn't leave clues and I didn't leave fingerprints or evidence and I sure as hell didn't take evidence with me.

But the hat was something. It meant something, it symbolized something.

The hat was a *reminder*. Call it a memory fragment, only one you could touch.

I had the strangest feeling I was going to need it.

I looked at the hat some more and the rain continued to fall and then I returned my attention to the yellow legal pad on my lap. I cast an optic down the page, skimming the small penciled writing to make sure I'd covered all the salient points, and then I pushed the button at the end of the mechanical pencil in my hand a couple of times and picked up where I'd left off.

I was on to something. I only had two problems.

One, if I was on to something then I had no idea what it was. I could only hope my notes would make some kind of sense to my newly awakened self in the morning.

Two, by making the notes I was breaking my own rules about not leaving clues. What I was writing was incriminating to say the least. Now I understood why the previous pages had been hidden. My only option, once I'd finished, was to do the same again.

I wondered how many times I had sat in the garage. How many times I had found out something I didn't really like. How many times I had written that down and then hidden the notes, just in case.

I reached the end of the page and then I reread what I had written and I thought I'd got it pretty well right. Then the telephone rang again and this time I picked it up but not before turning the legal pad upside down and sliding it underneath the black hat on the passenger seat. I wasn't entirely certain how much the party on the end of the line knew about what I was doing at any particular moment in time but having the pad out of my sight felt a good deal better.

I put the receiver against the side of my head and the empty line buzzed in my audio receiver. And then I heard her voice, loud and clear inside my head.

Ada let out a puff of electronic smoke from her imaginary cigarette and then her voice purred like movie star trying to get a free drink from a reluctant barman.

"Asleep at the wheel, Ray?"

I said nothing.

"You work too hard, chief," said Ada. "You could use a little shut-eye. Come up and see me."

I pursed my lips, or at least it felt like I did. I liked how it felt so I kept doing it for a second and then I said, "Sure, I'll be right up."

Ada made a noise you might take as approving and the line went dead. I put the telephone receiver back where I found it. I looked at the black hat on the passenger seat. I picked it up by the crown and turned it upside down and read the label. I thought about taking it with me and then I thought twice and I put it right back down on top of the notepad.

Then I turned the key in the ignition and the car growled and I backed out and I aimed for the rain.

I had about an hour left and I was going to use it. I knew I wouldn't remember a thing about tonight. Come the morning—well, come six o'clock—my world would start anew and I would be back to the proverbial square one.

But I had an idea. All I needed was that last hour of my day. And then I could forget about the hat and the legal pad and the job.

And I could forget everything I discovered about the late Touch Daley.

4

It was late when I finally reparked the car and made my way up the stairs into the office. But I had a few minutes to spare and if Ada knew anything was wrong I couldn't tell and she didn't sound any different from how she normally sounded.

But of course she knew. My little extra trip out hadn't been wasted. Far from it. It had confirmed what I had suspected.

Of course she knew.

But she knew something else too—that no matter what I had unearthed tonight, no matter what secrets had been revealed to me, I wouldn't remember a single thing in the morning.

Then again, I had a little secret or two of my own, and as I stood in the computer room behind the main office and I took off my hat, I couldn't help but feel my ohmmeter twinkle just a little at the thought of it.

Ada made a noise that might have been a sip of a very late cup of coffee but other than that there was only the whirr of her data tapes and the steady tick of her processor cores, the sound of the fast hand of a watch ticking ever onwards.

I put my hat on the small round table that stood in the middle of the back office and I slipped off my coat and put it over the back of the chair.

Then Ada lit a cigarette, or maybe she only did in some far distant recess of my computational comparison matrix, and she spoke at last.

"Busy night, chief," she said.

"You're telling me," I said.

Ada laughed. It was the laugh of a smoker and it echoed around the computer room a few times.

"Don't worry your pretty little head about it, Ray," she said when she was done. "A good night's sleep and everything will be just peachy pie, sweetie pie."

"Whatever you say, Ada," I said. I wasn't in the mood to argue and more than that I didn't have much time left. My priority was to get into my alcove and plug myself in and let the world fade away.

Was I the same person, when I woke up? Sure, I wasn't a *person*. As far as I knew, robots—even ones that looked like people—had only ever acquired the same legal rights as the automobile parked in the garage several floors underneath my feet. But I walked and I talked and I thought about things and I thought that made me a person of a kind.

But was I the same person when I woke up? Was the Ray Electromatic that was looking out of my optics at this very moment the same one that would be viewing the world in the morning? Or was he erased along with his tape, and another Ray Electromatic came along? Just the same as the original. Someone once said that we're the sum of our experiences and our memories. If I started each day with neither of those things, then what did that make me?

I got into my alcove and I put those thoughts out of my mind. My dynamic regression analyzer was churning away and getting a little hot for this late in my day.

I plugged myself into the main computer bank and I told myself not to worry about it. If this particular Ray Electromatic wasn't going to solve the mystery then maybe the next one would.

"It's the rain, isn't it?" asked Ada. "The weather. You never did like this kind of weather. It's not natural for Hollywood. This town runs on sunshine. I've always said so."

I lay back against the gentle slope of the alcove and looked up at the corner of the room where I more or less thought Ada was watching me from. I don't know why I thought that. There was no electric eye up there looking down on me but I just had a feeling in my diodes. On the two opposite sides of the room Ada's master computer banks hummed, the reel-to-reel tapes on them spinning slowly, the lights next to the tapes flashing in sequences that were meaningful but unknown to me. On the wall opposite my alcove was a window that looked out at the building opposite. There was no blind or shutter or curtain and with the lights on in the computer room and the sun yet to make an appearance the window was nothing but a dull black mirror.

I gave a shrug and I watched myself in the reflection. I looked insubstantial, transparent. A ghost in a machine.

"You're probably right there," I said.

"Uh-huh," said Ada. "Water and electricity—they don't mix. Water and *computers* don't mix. And that's what you are, Ray. A walking, talking computer."

She paused, and I had the feeling she was smoking again even though that was impossible.

"A walking, talking computer who is good with his hands," she said.

I sighed and it sounded like a low-flying jet traveling too slow.

And then the clock ticking over the main door clicked over to the hour and I woke up and it was another beautiful morning in Hollywood, California.

5

The morning sun poured in through the window in the office as I sat at the little round table in my shirtsleeves reading the newspaper. Ada's tapes spun around me and every now and again I'd look up and watch some lights flash and then I went back to my reading.

It was a nice morning. Quiet. I felt good. Ada was keeping to herself but I assumed she was busy working on the next job. That was fine. In the meantime I could sit and read the newspaper and learn about the state of the world, and as I read I thanked my previous self for being so thoughtful as to bring the early edition up when he had gone to bed. Reading the news was a good way of figuring out just what was going on in all that sunshine outside. One of the first things I did was have a quick shuffle through to see if I could find the name of the president. I figured that was a good baseline with which to start the day.

I found it on page four. President Kennedy was settling nicely into his second term and people seemed pretty pleased with how he was doing.

Good enough for me. Then I turned to the sports section and memorized a table of baseball results because I felt like it.

Ada was still busy doing hard sums so when I was done with the newspaper I folded it as neatly as I could and I stood up and went to the window. If I leaned a little to the right I could see past the brown brick building opposite and down to the street. There was a slice of brilliant blue sky above and people and cars moving down below and the world was turning and life went on and so far I didn't have much to do.

That was fine by me. Every minute standing by the window was another minute for our covertly invested finances to grow with interest. It occurred to me that with no job to do Ada was probably counting it all.

Everyone needs a hobby.

I picked up the newspaper and I unfolded it and refolded it and then I had the strangest notion that I could go out for a coffee and maybe a paperback novel if there wasn't anything else to do, and I was about to suggest the same to Ada even though I knew I couldn't drink coffee, when I heard the sound. It came from beyond the door that connected the computer room to the main office and it was the unmistakable announcement of someone coming in from the hallway and closing the main door behind themselves.

"Ada?" I asked.

"Look lively, chief," she said. "We've got company."

"So I gather."

I turned to face the door that led to the main office. Beyond that door was a large room with a polished wooden floor that was only partially covered by a thick rug. As far as my current memory tape went I'd never seen that room before in my life but I knew it was there all the same.

The sound of the outer door opening and closing was quickly followed by the sound of heavy footsteps crossing the office, not fast but not slow either, the owner of those particular shoes clearly on a mission to reach somewhere to sit. That somewhere was one of the two chairs in front of the desk that sat in front of the big louvered window. It was the kind of desk any self-respecting private detective would pilot, robotic or not, and had an appropriate amount of stationery arranged on the top along with a red leather blotter with just the right amount of wear and tear. The Electromatic Detective Agency might not be much involved in the detecting business anymore but looks were important.

The heavy footsteps became muffled as the potential client—one I would send packing, with the usual excuse that our books were full and maybe he could call again sometime next Christmas—hit the big rug, and then followed a series of other emanations consistent with someone pulling out a chair, sitting down in it, then adjusting the position just so.

"I'm assuming we're not expecting anyone?" I asked.

"The diary is wide open, chief," said Ada. "As it always is. You'd better get out there and find out what they want."

"As you say, boss."

I slipped my jacket from the back of the chair I had just been occupying and slipped it on. I left my hat where it was by the newspaper.

And then I walked up to the connecting door and opened it and stepped through it and then I closed it behind me.

The man in the chair looked up as I walked in and he gave me a smile that was as warm as a mortician's slab. He was a good-looking guy heading somewhere toward his fiftieth birthday. His strong jaw was clean shaven and his piercing eyes were as friendly as his expression. He had crossed his legs with one knee a good deal higher than looked comfortable. His hat was black and small, a trilby, and he held it with the fingers of one hand with the other hand folded underneath and he tapped it against his knee to a slow beat. The hat went rather well with his suit, which was also black, and with his hair, which was a dark oil slick that swept back from an impressive forehead.

I didn't know who he was but he looked like he meant business.

"Can I help you?" I asked, "Mister . . . ?"

"Daley. Touch Daley," said the visitor. "And as a matter of fact, Mr. Electromatic, I'm here to help *you*."

6

Mr. Touch Daley kept smiling and I didn't like it but with no moveable parts on my own face I didn't think he noticed. I stood by the closed door and watched him and he watched me. He had his head cocked, like he was trying to remember something. Maybe he was supposed to hit the grocery store on the way home but had forgotten what his wife said they needed.

I walked over to the desk as casual as you like and I grabbed the back of the big leather chair behind and swung it back and forth on the pivot a little. Then I looked at my prospective client and he was still looking at me from an angled neck. We played statues for a few more ticks of the clock but I knew that was a game I could easily win so I decided to break the ice again by telling him to get lost in as polite a way as I could muster.

"I don't normally take cold callers," I said, lowering

myself into my chair. When I was in place I put two bronzed titanium hands on the desk, fingers flat, and tapped them a little against the red leather blotter. I hoped he would get the picture. People coming into the office wasn't necessarily a bad thing. We were listed in the telephone directory and the number in the listing was real enough, as was the street address. The frosted glass of the door leading out into the building's hallway still had THE ELECTROMATIC DETECTIVE AGENCY stenciled on it in nice big gold lettering and on the wall inside the office were some framed certificates that showed my production date and system verification and my license from the City of Los Angeles. The license was up to date.

People could call us. Ada answered the telephone and told them we weren't taking new cases at the moment. She also took calls about other jobs we *were* taking, but they came in on an unlisted number. One of several, in fact. But the main office door was unlocked while I was there. People could come in. I would just have to show them out again.

The man sitting in the chair opposite me hadn't taken his eyes from my face and he didn't change his expression either, nor the angle of his head. But his hat bobbed only twice more on his knee and then was still and then he seemed to get more comfortable. The smile slowly faded but he didn't seem ready to do any more talking. He just sat and breathed and blinked.

I did none of those. I opened and closed the little flap that sat behind the grille of my mouth a couple of times and Mr. Daley watched me do it.

"Jobs the Electromatic Detective Agency takes on are of a very particular type," I said, "and I have to say my dance card is looking pretty full presently. But if you want to leave this office with your name and your number and perhaps a small idea of what it is I can do for you, then I can get my associates to call your associates and we can see what shakes out."

Mr. Daley watched me with firm lips that were now pursed and blue eyes that were now narrowed.

"On the other hand," I said, filling the air because the man in the other chair had apparently forgotten how to speak, "if you think you have information that I might find useful, I'd invite you to lay it out so we can take a good look and see what we've got."

Then his hat bounced on his knee again and finally the great Mr. Daley deigned to use his voice.

"You don't remember me, do you?" The corner of his mouth twitched up, like he was trying not to smile. I didn't like that any more than any other expression he had tried on in the three minutes I had known him.

"Can't say that I do," I said, which was entirely the truth. "But even if we've done business in the past, the moment you walk through that door we're back to square one. If it's a new job then we have a new agreement. I'm programmed for discretion and I have a talent for privacy, so you'll have to excuse me if I don't break out the cigars and brandy and yak about old times."

I thought that was pretty good. I sat back in my chair feeling pleased with myself. The fact was that nobody knew about the limitation of my memory tapes other than me and Ada.

At least as far as I knew.

"I remember you, Ray Electromatic."

"That is apparent, Mr. Daley."

The man's mouth twitched again like his smile needed a little kick-start, but a second later it was installed and shining as bright as the Alaskan sun.

"But as I said, Mr. Daley, if you think you can help me, by all means, let's hear it. Electronic I may be. Psychic was beyond the skills of my creator."

The hat bounced. Daley looked down at the rug. "Ah yes, Professor Thornton." Then his eyes came back up and the hat stilled. "That was a shame, wasn't it?"

I didn't know and that was also the truth, but I wasn't about to give Mr. Daley the pleasure, so I sat where I was and I kept my vocalizer unpowered.

"A shame about him, too, of course," said Mr. Daley.

That was when the telephone on the desk next to my right arm began to ring. Mr. Daley glanced at it and smiled and he watched it like it was his favorite TV show. I watched him watch and then I said, "Excuse me," and I picked up the receiver. I knew who it was.

"Get rid of him, Ray."

"You talking in a permanent or temporary sense?"

"You sit behind that desk and the power goes to your head, chief," said Ada. "Temporary. His person and your office need to be separated by a distance, the farther the better."

I rotated the mouthpiece away from my face and looked at Daley and he just nodded and smiled and got to work juggling his hat again. I moved the mouthpiece back to where it had been before.

"Is there something in particular you wanted to talk to me about right now?"

"Your illustrious client is trouble, Raymondo. Whatever you do, don't listen to him."

"That's two things to do. I'll need to make a list."

"Just shut him up and ship him out, Ray. Trust me on this one. Nothing Touch Daley says is anything you need to pay attention to. Are we clear?"

"As crystal," I said, and then I put the phone down.

Daley jerked his chin at me. "Your . . . *associate*?"

I didn't like his tone. I frowned, or at least I tried to. I was doing it on the inside and I had a feeling Touch Daley probably knew it.

"You'll have to excuse me, Mr. Daley, but my schedule is full and I have matters to attend to. But thanks for coming by. This conversation was real swell. We should get together again sometime and not talk about anything."

Daley nodded and made to get up. I stood and then waited because Daley was only half out of the chair when he stopped and he sighed and then he continued on his way to the full upright. He winced, like he was in pain, and he pointed at me with his hat, which he held out by the crown.

"She's a real good gal," he said. "It was such a shame about her, but then you wouldn't know anything about that either, would you?"

"Walking into offices and talking in riddles is a hell of a hobby you have there, Mr. Daley. You ever thought about collecting cigarette cards instead?"

"Oh, no, I came here for a reason, don't worry." He put his hat on and looked thoughtful about it. "I was speaking the truth when I said I was here to help you." He paused and looked at the rug while he contemplated the infinite. "Actually, I came here to tell you something very—"

The telephone rang again. Daley stopped speaking and watched the telephone and he watched my hand reach for it, but I didn't pick it up. It rang on and I didn't know why I let it but I did. I stood there and Daley looked at the phone and then he looked at me.

"I'm listening," I said. "Say what you want and then you'd better get out. My *associate* needs me to go and get coffee and her magazine, and you know what they're like when they haven't done their morning crossword puzzle."

Daley nodded and he opened his mouth to raise his voice over the ringing phone, but I held up a hand and he stopped mid-breath.

"I can hear you just fine."

Daley's jaw clicked shut and he nodded like he knew what I meant. And then he glanced at the connecting door and then glanced back at me and he gave another nod and I knew that he did.

"I'm here to give you a warning."

"Keep going."

"Trouble is coming."

"Trouble is my business."

Daley shook his head. "Not trouble like this. You're going to be in danger, and very soon."

"Don't tell me, you're the only one who can get me out of it?"

"Not at all. I have some . . . *associates* . . . of my own being mobilized as we speak. In fact, there's a chance we might not meet again, although if we don't then you'll know that things aren't going to plan. But there are others who will be coming to help. You'd be wise to let them."

I processed this information for a few seconds. The

telephone continued to ring. Touch Daley looked at me and then he looked at the telephone and then he nodded again and he put his hat on his head.

"I'll see you again, I hope," he said, and then he headed for the door. He paused again, and when he spoke he addressed his words to the door without turning around.

"Check the spare wheel."

Then he resumed his progress toward the exit. I didn't move. I just stood where I was and I watched him cross the office and leave it. His outline was visible through the frosted glass of the door after he closed it behind him, and I watched as he paused and seemed to check his direction before heading to the right, toward the elevator.

The telephone continued to ring but I let it. I went back to the computer room. I wanted to talk to Ada in person.

7

As soon as I crossed the threshold from one office to the other the telephone on the desk stopped ringing. I stood in the doorway for a moment and gave the computer room a quick scan. Lights flashed on Ada's consoles and mainframe banks and maybe it was my imagination but they seemed a little brighter than they had been earlier. Ada's big reel-to-reel tapes spun this way and that and the tape snapped and whirred and the air was filled with a quiet burbling, like a tea kettle coming to a boil, as a million microswitches switched back and forth behind her shiny white panels. The clock above the door ticked onwards.

I let the door close and I moved back to the little round table.

"Anything you want to tell me, Ada?"

"Nothing you don't already know, chief."

I nodded. I reached down and moved my hat a little.

"Considering I don't know anything from before an hour ago, save what the *Hollywood Daily News* has to say about current events, I'm not entirely sure that answers my question."

Ada paused. It felt like she was holding her breath, or at least it felt like that somewhere inside my positronic brain. A moment later and that feeling was gone as the electrons that moved through my circuits got on with more important things.

"Trust me, chief," she said. "There's nothing you need to worry about."

I pursed my lips. I was getting better at it.

"Touch Daley," I said.

"What about him?"

"I've met him before, I take it."

One tape reel slammed to a halt, then reversed direction. The noise of it was something of a surprise.

"Ada?"

"Yes, Ray, you have met Touch Daley before. But trust me, it wasn't an encounter worth remembering. He's a nobody. Forget about him."

A nobody I had met before, who knew who I was and who knew about my "associate" Ada. A nobody who seemed to know something about Professor Thornton. Maybe even what had happened to him.

A nobody who had taken the time to come and give me a warning, in person.

But Ada was right when she told me to forget about him, because I knew I would, after today. By this time tomorrow Touch Daley would be a stranger once more.

Had Touch Daley been to the office before? Did he come every morning? Had we had that very same conversation every morning for the last six months? Somehow I doubted it. A warning tends to lose its urgency just a little if you have to keep giving it each day.

So we'd met before but this was probably his first visit to the office. Maybe he had warned me before, somewhere else. Only he thought I wasn't listening, so he had taken steps and come to the office.

I wondered how much Ada had heard. I decided not to ask her. It didn't matter. I may not have known a thing about my previous meetings with Mr. Daley, but Ada did. Everything that was on my memory tapes was in her memory banks, and they were all permanent ones. That was partly why she was the size of an office.

Check the spare wheel.

Well. Maybe I would. I wondered if Ada knew what that meant. I decided not to ask her about that either. Not yet, anyway.

Ada's lights flashed and now they seemed to be dimmer, and her tapes spun and they seemed to spin slower. I moved to the table and I made a show of picking up the newspaper and opening it and straightening the pages up. A moment later I thought I heard the click of a metal teaspoon against a ceramic mug and I thought I could smell coffee being brewed somewhere close by, but I knew I was mistaken so I ignored it.

I stood by the window and I read a story about the mysterious death of a real estate magnate but I didn't take it in. I was too busy replaying the conversation with Touch Daley. I wished I'd taken a snap or two of him with the cameras that sat behind my optics.

Then there were two sharp clicks. I lowered the newspaper.

"Okay, Ray," said Ada, sounding like she'd just finished the last hot gulp from her mug and was working up to make a start on the next cigarette in the line. "Time for you to get to work."

"Glad to hear it," I said. I put the newspaper down and I picked up my hat. In the corner of the room a thin ribbon of ticker tape began its dive toward the floor from the slot in the computer bank as Ada printed off my instructions. I walked over and held the paper between my hands as it continued to crawl from the slot.

I looked up into the corner of the room. "Bay City?"

"Bay City," said Ada.

I pursed my lips, or at least it felt like I did. "That's a little out of the way."

"It's a nice place," said Ada. "Classy. The sunshine will be good for your circuits. I hear they have a lot of it out there."

The ticker-tape machine stopped. I tore the strip off, read it again, then curled it up and slipped it into my pocket.

Then I put my hat on and headed for the door.

"Send me a postcard!" said Ada, but I was already gone and I was thinking about other things.

8

Ada was right. After taking myself and my car west through Hollywood and then Beverly Hills and on toward the coast, I discovered that Bay City was indeed a neighborhood with a certain kind of class. The sunshine sure didn't hurt. We had sunshine in the rest of Los Angeles but here the sunshine felt like it was in a different class too. Maybe it was the nice big houses the place seemed full of. Maybe it was the view of the bay itself as I pulled into a beachside parking lot to get my bearings. Beyond the rail of the lot and the slope of the sand the ocean was a vast and flat expanse of blue so deep some might even be tempted to call it azure.

Myself, I settled on blue as good enough. I turned the car off and I sat there with the window down and the breeze coming in and cooling down the inside of the car. That was as good for my circuits as the sunshine was, because since walking out of the office and getting in my car in the garage, those circuits had been doing a lot of work and my electronics were getting a hell of a baking. I was a robot and that meant I didn't get headaches, but Professor Thornton sure must have because right then my head felt like someone had an industrial vice and was applying it liberally across my temples.

I put one bronzed titanium alloy elbow on the doorframe and enjoyed the cool sea breeze for a moment and then I turned and looked down at the object that was giving me that headache. It sat on the passenger seat and I hadn't touched it. It had been there when I had gotten into the car and there it still lay.

It was a hat. It had a folded crown and a narrow brim that curled toward the rear. I would have called it a trilby. It was black and I could tell just by looking at it that even if it was my style, which it wasn't, it was a good deal too small for my own cranium.

But about the right size for Touch Daley. In fact, I would have said the hat was his, apart from the fact that he had been wearing it in the office when I last saw him. Or at least he had been clutching it with those long fingers of his. It was a sensible hat and quite smart too and it went with his suit and the more I thought about it the less likely it seemed that, after our little meeting not an hour ago, he had gone down into the garage and found my car and opened it with keys of his own and placed the hat there for me to find.

The hat didn't sit well on either of my primary or secondary resonating voltage wafers.

I sat there looking at the ocean and looking at the hat and then I did what any good detective would do when confronted with a mystery. I investigated. And I started by picking up the hat. I examined it. It was a nice hat and not a cheap one either. I turned it over. The band around the edge was a little worn but not too much. There was nothing inside the hat except that sea breeze. I held it by the crown and flipped the band inside out. There was nothing there either.

I went to put the hat back where I had found it and that's when I found my second clue. Because sitting on the passenger seat underneath the hat was a single sheet of yellow lined paper, a page of something like a legal pad. With the hat in one hand I picked up the paper and I let it fall open along the fold and I read what was inside it.

It wasn't much. Two lines of nothing much, in fact.

The second line was an address.

The first line was an instruction. It read:

GO HERE INSTEAD.

Both lines were written in mechanical pencil in a handwriting I recognized immediately on account of it being my own.

I rested the note on one knee and the hat on the other and I looked out at the ocean. It was lunchtime and the beach was doing reasonable business considering it was a weekday. Bay City seemed to have enough of a population of those lucky enough not to heed the demands of the nine to five that they could take advantage of the sun when it shone, which was often, and the water when it shimmered and glittered and lay as flat as a pool table, which was always. I was just a robot in his car minding his business and taking in the view and nobody seemed to mind that too much.

I decided I liked Bay City.

The hat I liked a little less. The note, forget about it. I didn't want to talk about that note.

But it did give me a clue about what I should do next.

Ada had sent me on a job. She had given me a name and an address and those details were sitting on the little strip of ticker tape that was rolled up and inside my jacket pocket. I had no further instructions but I knew what I was doing. I'd wasted no time in getting to Bay City despite the fact it was daylight. My line of work was one that required discretion and secrecy and not getting caught, and daylight was often something of a hindrance. But that didn't mean I had to sit and watch the sea all day, even if that seemed like it would be nice. No, what I had to do now was not entirely unlike what Professor Thornton had programmed me for. Being a private detective was a good cover but it also equipped me with a certain set of skills that came in useful.

All I had was a name and an address and Ada trusted me to get on with the rest of it. What she didn't know was that I had apparently preempted myself and left the note with the other address, which was also in Bay City.

If there was one thing I didn't believe in, it was coincidences.

So I looked at the ocean and I looked at the note and I decided that the Raymond Electromatic of yesterday probably knew what he was talking about and that the Raymond Electromatic of today would do well to trust him.

Call it . . . self-employment. I was on a case of my own devising and I was my own client.

I liked that.

But first I had another little job to do: I was going to get out of the car and take a look under the spare wheel in the trunk like Mr. Touch Daley had suggested.

I folded the note and I put it in my pocket. I put the hat back on the passenger seat. Then I pulled the brim of my own down a little more over my optics. I took the keys out of the ignition and I opened my door and I closed it with a metallic crunch that was both satisfying and quite possibly audible from the office back in West Hollywood. But I was out in the open with nothing to hide, so I hid nothing. As I walked around to the back of my Buick a couple of people strolled past on the boardwalk that abutted the parking lot and only one pair of eyes even looked in my direction.

I'd done enough thinking so I didn't waste any more time on it. I slipped the car key into the lock of the trunk, gave it a twist, and pulled the lid up.

The trunk was empty. The floor was a carpeted board with a little canvas pull tag. It didn't look like it had been disturbed, but then I wasn't sure if I expected it to be or not.

I checked to see who was around me and there were several people but none of them showed me any interest. But it didn't hurt any to play it cool. I had the strangest feeling that there was something going on in the world and I didn't know what it was. Call it an ache, a kind of dull throb that ran down the diodes on one side of my chassis and back up the other.

Because if there was something going on, I had known about it—yesterday.

I leaned over like anyone would and I pulled the pull tag and I lifted the floor of the trunk. There was a spare wheel underneath and some tools in a sort of leather holster. I lifted the wheel. There was nothing underneath it. I checked the wheel itself. There was nothing hidden inside the rim, and the tire itself was intact and inflated to what felt like the correct pressure. Then I put the wheel back and I unbuckled the holster of tools and laid it out along the top of the wheel. I had everything there to switch one wheel for another and I had to admire Buick for their attention to detail as every tool was embossed with the make and model of my car. It was a very nice set of tools, but there was nothing there that a reasonable motorist would not expect to find in their trunk and there wasn't anything hidden either.

I stood with the sunshine on my back as I pondered the results of my investigation and the advice Touch Daley had given me in the office. His words had been simple and hardly open to interpretation, but there was nothing here. Maybe Ada was right and there was nothing that Touch Daley said that was worth listening to.

Including warnings of imminent peril.

The four wheels of the car currently *in situ* were doing just fine so I wrapped up the tools and I put them back and I slid the floor of the trunk back into the car but no matter what I did, it wouldn't lay flat. I tried a few times then gave up.

I stopped and looked at it awhile and then I thought again about that something going on. Maybe it was just paranoia. Or maybe that was the human condition I'd heard so much about. I didn't know. I was a robot who couldn't remember what he'd had for lunch yesterday. The human condition was a little beyond my purview.

I closed the trunk and strolled around to the driver's door and slipped back inside the car. It was still hot. Hotter, perhaps, now that the cool sea breeze had died and the air was left to sit just where it was and get lightly broiled by that famous Bay City sun.

I reached into the pocket of my coat. I took out the strip of ticker tape. I read the name and the address that was on it.

Then I took out the folded sheet of note paper with the other address and the instruction.

GO HERE INSTEAD.

Then I put both back into my pocket and I started the car and backed out of the lot and got back onto the street and as I drove toward the address on the notepaper I hoped that the information the Raymond Electromatic of yesterday had acquired was a little more useful than the vague suggestions of the mysterious Mr. Touch Daley.

9

I didn't know where the address on the yellow note was going to lead me but I found it soon enough, on a quiet street a few blocks down from the beach. The building in question wasn't residential although it was in a block that was a mix of houses and storefronts. It was largish and neatly rectangular in a way that suggested the architect was either an aficionado of European minimalism or desperately bored by his work. The whole construction was set back from the street to make room for a parking lot, the rear half of which the building loomed over as it rode a parade of columns that were anything but Greco-Roman. The section of the building thus supported had very big windows high up and they were all open. From within came the sound of activity.

It sounded like I'd come to some kind of health club. Maybe a small, private gymnasium.

I took all this in as I pulled into the lot and then I turned the car around as I eased into a slot, so I was left facing the street rather than the building. I liked to do that. It seemed less obvious than sitting there staring dead ahead.

I killed the engine and looked into the rearview just as a middle-aged man with wet gray hair came out of the main doors hidden between all those columns. He was wearing a navy-blue track suit with a red stripe down the leg and he had a red towel slung over one shoulder and a canvas bag slung over the other. The canvas bag was long enough to carry a guitar. Maybe he was the in-sauna entertainment.

More sounds emanated from the high windows. The sounds were of movement punctuated with a light, metallic clattering and the squeak of rubber-soled shoes on a polished floor and there was periodic shouting coupled with a periodic buzzing like the intercom in a doctor's waiting room in a bad part of town.

Despite all the noise, the place seemed to be having a quiet spell, at least going by the number of cars in the lot. It was mid-afternoon and a hot one at that. Maybe everyone else was down at the beach. That sounded like the better option and I didn't even swim.

I got out of the car and locked it and stood for a moment looking at the other vehicles keeping mine company. There was nothing much to speak of, except for one big German number, a silver sedan with a hood long enough for the hundred-yard dash and an ornament on the radiator cap that was shaped like a trefoil and rose up like a gun target. The car was unusual and expensive and polished to a good shine.

I stood by my car for a moment and I looked at the other

car and I listened to the symphony of activity from within the building. Then I ventured through the columns and went inside.

I found myself in a lobby that was devoid of any life and that had a desk at the end behind a glass divider. There was a cork noticeboard on my left and a set of stairs on my right and a big set of double doors somewhere between them. The doors had little square windows in them reinforced with a wire mesh.

I headed left.

The noticeboard was divided into four named sections and was covered with pinned papers. The second section had a fancier name panel than the others, a thing of dark wood and gold letters more in keeping with a firm of lawyers than a gym club.

Or perhaps a firm of private detectives. I looked at the letters and wondered if the same guy had done the notice on the door of my office.

The panel said BAY CITY FENCING CLUB and the notices beneath it were a list of members with a column for a check mark and something about their annual Christmas dance.

I took one long look down the list of members and then I took Ada's ticker tape out of my pocket and took a somewhat shorter look down that. I didn't need to. I knew every letter printed on it. But I did it all the same and then I read the list of members again. There was no match but I wasn't sure if I expected there to be. I was trusting my past self on this one.

Satisfied I had interrogated the noticeboard, I went to the big double doors but I didn't open them. There was no sound from beyond and when I looked through the square wired windows all I saw was an empty gym. I pulled one of the door handles in an experimental fashion and found it was locked.

It seemed all the action was happening upstairs. So I turned right and took the stairs up one level where I found myself in a smaller lobby with a smaller set of double doors. The sounds were louder and when I tried the left-hand door it swung open without protest.

It was another gym, this one a good deal larger than the one downstairs on account of the extension that advanced out over half the parking lot. The room was predominantly yellow in color. It had bleacher seats rising along one wall and various rope-based apparatus hanging from the ceiling. There were small trampolines stacked upright against the far wall and two pommel horses likewise pushed out of the way of what was going on in the middle of the hall, which was nothing short of one-on-one combat.

There were two long strips taped to the floor, twenty yards long and five wide. Next to each, in the middle, was a trestle table with a box on it with lights. Each box had a power cord that was taped to the floor as they ran out along the room to the outlets on the wall.

I counted six people in total taking part in the sport—four engaged in bouts, two acting as referees. They were all dressed in white, with short breeches and long socks, and jackets with high collars.

The Bay City Fencing Club was in full flow.

The four fencers on the pistes were wearing masks fronted with white mesh that hid their faces, and from the backs of their jackets trailed a wire leading to a spool that sat at either end of the pistes. As the fencers fenced, their weapons clattered against each other, occasionally ringing off an opponent's guard like a hammer striking a bell. The men bounced up and down and back and forth and their shoes squeaked on the strips as they tried their damnedest to keep out of reach of their opponent's weapon.

With everyone so engaged I stood by the door unnoticed. I watched awhile. There was a kind of beauty in it, a ballet as the combatants danced up and down their strips, parrying their opponents, riposting, attacking, defending. Quite often the attacks were successful and resulted in a buzzing sound and a light from the box on the trestle table and a cry of delight from the man who had landed a hit. Fists were raised and masked heads were shaken and then the referee called them back to the *en garde* position, sometimes after a not insubstantial conversation in French.

To my surprise I was able to follow the action without too much difficulty. I checked my permanent store and found a rule book. I guess Professor Thornton had liked fencing too. I could see why. It was a good way to keep fit, and there was also a romance to it as well as a kind of beauty. I knew that fencing was a sport like any other and they even had it at the Olympics along with swimming and running and other more commonplace efforts. But fencing was different somehow. Some—fencers, most likely—might even call it sophisticated.

What it certainly was was *expensive*. I looked over the gear and checked the time. It was four-thirty on a Wednesday afternoon and there was only a certain portion of the population who could spend a workday afternoon trying to poke a metal stick into their fellow enthusiasts.

Soon enough one bout finished and the fencers shook

hands and took off their masks before heading to the bleachers to towel off. One of them saw me, and after first disconnecting the cable that ran from the cuff of his jacket into the socket of his épée, and then the cable from the back of his jacket to the spool on the floor, he rubbed his face again with his towel and swung the towel over his neck and padded over in his gym shoes. He was an older fellow with a handlebar moustache and enough gray at his temples to look impressive in the boardroom. There was a broadness to his forehead. I imagined the brain behind it was full of numbers and stock prices and share grants and other things I imagined rich executives knew a lot about.

As he approached he looked me up and down like he was appreciating a fine painting. I didn't know whether I should have been flattered or not. He was clearly old enough to remember a time when there had been robots, some of them like me and some of them not. A man like him, somewhere high up the food chain, he probably saw robots and people the same way. Just tools for the job, whether it was polishing his shoes or mowing his lawn or driving him to his high-rise office in downtown LA.

I touched the brim of my hat with a finger and did my best to look casual, which was not a lot considering I couldn't change the expression on my face. As soon as the moustache and the fencer it was attached to came within an acceptable distance for conversation, he grabbed the two ends of the towel around his neck like he was about to jump out of an airplane.

"Can I help you?" he asked.

"Fencing's a nice game," I said, leaning back into the door and folding my arms. "Always thought so." And that was true, given that I hadn't thought of fencing before a quarter hour ago and I'd liked it as soon as I had.

"Fencing, my friend, is a *martial art*," said the man with lips that moved and a moustache that stayed put. "An ancient and historic sport that had its home in the royal courts of Europe for centuries."

It seemed I was right about fencers. I pursed my lips, or I would have.

"But what can I help you with?" asked the moustache that was less a soup catcher and more a safety net for an all-you-can-eat buffet. "Something tells me you are not here to enquire about club membership."

Behind him the other bout had finished up and the two fencers and the referee had joined the other two at the bleachers. They were all looking at us although they were too far away for them to hear what we were saying. Not that it was much of a conversation. "You might be right there," I said, "although you never know, maybe I'd be good at it. I wouldn't need the mask, after all."

The mouth under the moustache chuckled in a way that indicated the owner of both did not find what I had said amusing.

"Actually, I'm looking for someone," I said.

"Is that so?" His eyes narrowed and I got the feeling that maybe he knew something and I didn't.

It was a feeling I was getting more of all the time and I didn't like it much. It made my voltage comparators skip a megacycle or two.

"Friend of mine," I said. "Thought I'd meet him for lunch. His secretary told me he'd be here."

The tip of the man's tongue appeared for a moment

through the gray hedgerow hanging from his upper lip and then he half-turned back toward the bleachers. Most of the gang were in quiet conversation, no longer interested in what was going on between me and the moustache at the door.

All except the guy at the back. His mask was still in place and he wasn't talking to his friends.

He'd made a mistake. Because the bout had finished and the gym was hot and his buddies were cooling off. The only reason he was still wearing the mask was because he knew who I was and, more important, who I was looking for.

Which was him. He was my guy. He had to be.

The man with the moustache turned back around. "Something of a late lunch."

I shrugged. "This is Los Angeles. Every lunch is a late lunch."

His eyebrows came together and did a passable impression of the fuzz under his nose. "Somebody sent you, right?"

Before I could answer he sighed and his moustache trembled like a thin curtain in an evening breeze. Then he lowered his head and took a step forward.

"Listen, chum, this is a private club, okay?" he said to my shoes. He lifted his head up a little. "And we don't appreciate the invasion, okay?" He said that to my middle button. "So you can just get out and stay out and tell your editor that he's going to get some very important phone calls that he's not going to enjoy very much, okay?"

"My editor?"

Now the head came up and the moustache came with it. The ends of it stood out an inch from the sides of his face and I watched a drop of sweat coalesce on the very tip on the left side.

"The *Los Angeles Times*. The *Hollywood Daily News*. The *Bay City Real Estate Monthly*. Whatever rag it is you work for, I won't have my club members harassed in this manner."

I didn't point out that the only person in the club being harassed at that moment was me and I wasn't even a member.

"You think I'm a reporter?"

"There would be some inclined to disagree with you," he said, "but if you want to call yourself that, chum, then be my guest."

I let a couple of processor cycles run by. I looked at the guy again. He was old enough to remember robots, which meant he was old enough to know what had happened to them.

"You think they have robot reporters now? In 1965?"

The man snarled as a sudden spark of anger somewhere inside him caught light. "I wouldn't put anything past the *Hollywood Daily News*. That paper isn't fit to line my cat's litter tray with. Listen, chum, your editor is a schmuck and until today I thought he'd tried it all. You just go back to him and tell him I know what's what."

"Listen," I said, "I don't know what you're talking about. I haven't even told you who I'm looking for."

The smile returned and it was a smile that told me to get the hell back to my editor and explain how I'd annoyed someone important on the LA business roundtable. If only I'd had an editor. I thought Ada would do in a pinch, but I before I reported back to her about the incredible facial hair I had met and the angry man who owned it I needed to get some kind of information worth reporting.

The fencer was getting hotter under that white tunic of his. "Well?"

I told him the name that was printed on the ticker tape.

The man's smile widened and he showed some teeth. It was the smile of a man ready to throw a punch. His teeth were very white but they were a little crooked at the front.

"Get the hell out," he said, and he said it very quietly and then he lowered his head and he repeated the instruction, this time to my shoes. If I'd known they were going to be spoken to twice in one day I would have got them polished on the way in.

"The charm of your establishment overwhelms me," I said.

The man folded his arms, and half-turned to his friends again. The one in the mask was gone. There was a door at the back of the gym, leading, I assumed, to the locker room. I hadn't seen or heard him leave but I'd been a little preoccupied.

"Get the hell out," said the man again, "or so help me I'll call the police."

"I get the picture," I said, "although I'm not sure you have."

I turned and left the guy steaming under his moustache. Once the double doors were safely closed behind me I paused and considered the events of the day. Clearly they'd had trouble with reporters turning up in the past. Although quite why reporters would come to the Bay City Fencing Club was beyond me.

But I'd found my guy. The name on Ada's ticker tape wasn't on the noticeboard downstairs, but the club manager had known it. That was because the target *was* a member—the man who hadn't taken his mask off—he just used a different name for the club roster. That seemed like a strange thing to do, but then this was Los Angeles so I knew better to question it.

Now *there* was some detective work.

The only problem was that my target knew not only that I was looking for him but also who I was and what I did for pocket money, otherwise there would have been no reason for him to keep his face disguised and sneak out the back without so much as a farewell to his friends. My bet was that my target was already down in the parking lot.

I wasted no further time and headed down the stairs two at a time. On the ground level the lobby was still empty. I crossed the space and went out into the parking lot.

And then I stopped, because a voice called out. I turned to my left, and there he was, standing behind one of the pillars that supported the gym floor above. He was still in his white gear but had lost the mask. He leaned his upper body out from behind the pillar and he jerked his head like he wanted me to come over, so I did. I didn't know what was going on, and other than his name I didn't know who he was or what he had done to get on someone's hit list. That wasn't my problem. But I did know that I had a job to do and that fraternizing with the target wasn't a commonplace technique for an assassination. Ada was going to be four kinds of angry about what I was about to do.

Which was to walk over to the man behind the pillar and stop and ask him a question.

"Fresco Peterman, I presume?"

The man frowned like he'd never heard the name before. He was handsome in a way that got you onto the cover of a magazine. His hair was swept back in a fetching wave and he had a chin you could cut glass with. His eyes were small and they were blue and they squinted at me from out of the shadows of the pillar.

"Listen, Sparks, you can't come waltzing in there like that. People will talk, Ray. This town is built on chatter."

I stopped where I was, which was between two pillars. Out on the street beyond the parking lot cars came and went.

Fresco Peterman grinned. "Ah, don't worry about it, Sparks. You were just using your initiative. Don't tell me, a little note to yourself hidden in the glove box?"

I cast a glance at the street. I felt a little exposed where I was, a big robot in a big coat talking to what would look like nothing more than an ugly concrete pillar from the street.

"Actually, it was on the passenger seat," I said.

Peterman jerked his head back like he'd touched his nose to the terminal of a battery and he barked out a laugh.

For a second there I saw myself holding my hand out in a dark loud room and watching as a blue spark crackled on one fingertip and a small flame flared and a man leaned back with a cigarette smoldering between his lips. And then the image was gone and I was back in the parking lot with a guy I was supposed to kill and I could have sworn he was the man with the cigarette in that dark loud room.

"Hey, good for you, Sparks," said Peterman when he had recovered. "Good for you."

I didn't know what to say so I said nothing. Peterman licked his lips and then leaned back, ducking out from the pillar to look at the street.

"Listen, okay, we gotta talk, yes? But not here. Okay? I know a place. I'll go. You follow. You keep it discreet, okay? We got eyes watching all over the show." Peterman narrowed his eyes at me again. "You got that, Ray?"

I could already hear the telephone ringing in my parked car. I turned and listened to it for a while. Peterman heard it too, because he looked, and then he nodded, perhaps to himself. Then he stepped out of shadow of the pillar and got close enough to give my arm a slap. He did it too hard and hissed as his hand made contact and then he shook it in the air like that would make it better.

Then he said "come on," and he walked into the parking lot and got into the big German sedan and turned it on and he left the lot. Out on the street he indicated the wrong way and then pulled over. He wound down a window and waved his arm at me and then the arm went back inside and the car roared and rocked on its suspension as he blasted off down the street.

I didn't know who he was but I sure as hell wanted to find out so I got into my car and I ignored the ringing phone and I followed Fresco Peterman back into the city.

10

I kept myself at an inconspicuous distance from Fresco Peterman's big German number like any private detective worth his salt. Peterman had said that there were eyes on him, which I assumed also meant eyes on me. So I took it easy and I think I did a pretty good job.

Peterman did a good job too. I didn't know who he was but he knew what he was doing. After leaving the gym he wove around Bay City and then he headed east and for a while there I thought he was heading toward my neck of the woods. But then he turned again and cut a zigzag path all over the western reaches of Los Angeles and soon enough we were winding up into the hills with the sky some more of that azure blue above and the city slowly baking in a shimmering haze below. After a while there was a little traffic and then there was none so I decided to ditch any pretense that I wasn't on someone's tail and I got in close. If anyone was following us now it had to be in an invisible car, and if anyone saw us I thought they probably deserved to.

We drove more and soon the hills surrounded us and it felt like we were on another planet, not merely in the dusty edge of the desert right on the angels' doorstep. I wound my window down and smelled live oak and wild sage and that peculiar tang of hot places that made my circuits zip. If Ada could only have bottled that smell and sold it downtown we might have been in another line of work altogether.

I liked it up here, out of the city. I didn't know if I'd been up here before, but if I had I knew I would have liked it just as much then as I did now. It was hot and dry and scrubby but there was life up here. Birds and other animals and trees that were surprisingly green and vital.

Then I realized I'd backed off a little as I took in the surrounds and I couldn't see Peterman's car, just the comet tail of dust his tires were doing a good job of kicking up. I pushed the accelerator and kicked up my own plume and after another crest or two the one I was chasing began to die. When it cleared I saw Peterman parked under some of those live oaks. I pulled up behind him and turned the engine off and sat and listened to birdsong and the ticking of two hot cars. We were in a sort of basin filled with old trees. It was cooler here and there was a nice breeze coming in.

I could see Peterman's silhouette as he sat in his car. He hadn't moved from the driver's seat but he was looking around, one arm over the back of the seat, his eyes behind a pair of large sunglasses of the type favored by pilots. He was checking the road, making sure we really were alone. He seemed to be doing a good job so I left him to it.

As I watched him I considered that he was my target, and that I had a job to do, and that Mr. Fresco Peterman had very kindly led me to the particular kind of locale that was rather suitable for the kind of work I engaged in. We were alone and the road was empty and the trunk of Peterman's sedan looked plenty big enough to fold him into. On the way up we'd passed a good handful of ravines and some of them looked pretty handy, the kind that were almost triangular, the sides steep and stony and awkward, the base scrubby and prone to night patrols of coyotes. Hell, even the Hollywood sign wasn't too far away, and I'd always thought those letters were big enough for someone to take a fall that would make the police shake their heads and take off their caps and lament the toll the City of Angels took on some of its more vulnerable inhabitants.

But I also knew something else.

I wasn't going to do the job.

At least . . . not yet. Because Fresco Peterman wasn't just a name handed to me by Ada. He knew who I was and he knew I was coming to find him. He knew about the note, which meant he knew about the limitations of my memory.

I had a feeling I knew him just as well as he knew me, only I didn't remember.

It was time to renew that acquaintance.

Apparently satisfied that the coast was clear, Peterman swung the door of his car open. It was heavy and bounced on its hinges and his arm came out to stop it closing again. From where I sat I could see he was fussing with something. Then he got out and I could see it was a cigarette lighter that wouldn't light the cigarette that was now sticking straight out of his mouth. With the door still open he leaned back against the car and worked on the lighter. Somewhere on the journey over he'd managed to get out of the fencing jacket and he stood there in a white T-shirt and short white pants with long white socks and white gym shoes.

I got out of my car. I closed the door. I stopped and stood and listened to the birds and I smelled the smell of the desert and then I walked over to where Peterman was ignoring me.

"Damn thing," he said, finally giving up on the lighter but not before giving it a good shake. He sighed around his cigarette and tossed the lighter into the car. Then he looked around at the trees and the scrub, his cigarette lifting in the air as the lips around it moved into a frown like he was surprised there wasn't a whole bunch of lighters growing on the tree by the car.

"Here," I said. I reached forward with one hand. Peterman got the drift because although he was still frowning he moved his head down and he poked it out so the cigarette was pointing at me. I shorted a solenoid and a blue spark jumped from my fingertip to the end of his cigarette. Peterman puffed and then leaned back and blew smoke into the warm air with the sense of a man truly appreciating the world around him.

"Sparks, you're a life saver."

I glanced back at my car, half-expecting the telephone to start ringing, but there was no sound except the birds in the trees and the wind sweeping up the sandy dirt and depositing it on my loafers.

"Good job last night, Ray," said Peterman, working on

his cigarette as he spoke. "Thought that storm was going to make things difficult, but it was a big help, right?"

I turned back to him. Not for the first time I wished I had more than a twenty-four-hour memory tape. All I could do was reset a logic gate or two and hope he was going to fill me in.

Peterman froze, two fingers around his cigarette, eyes open and staring, cheeks in the processing of sucking in another lungful. He stood like that for a few seconds. The wind tugged on his T-shirt but somehow not his hair, which shone with something a little stronger than tonic. Wood varnish, I would have guessed.

"Oh yeah," he said, mostly to himself. "Right. No problem. We did a good job. Trust me. Nice and tidy." Then he coughed and he took the cigarette out of his mouth and then he put it back in and took another draw even as he was still coughing on the first one. "Mind you, we've had some practice at it now. We make a good team, you and me, Sparks. A good team."

If I could have frowned I would have, but I got the feeling Peterman got the idea. He took another look at me and he shook his head and he tossed his just-lit cigarette into the dirt. I watched it continue to smoke.

"I'll have to take your word on that," I said. "Call it a design flaw. All I can hold is—"

"Twenty-four hours of memory," said Peterman. "I know, I got it." He pointed two fingers at my chest like he was still holding his cigarette. "High-density magnetic tape, one-eighth inch, micro-monolith recording heads with a five-minute redundancy. One of Thornton's most overlooked achievements, and that's saying something, considering everything else the prof did."

There was a little flap behind my mouth grille. It didn't have much of a function except, perhaps, to keep dust out of my vocalizer, which was useful up here on the hills. But other than that it wasn't really necessary. It opened when I spoke and it closed when I didn't and it did so silently. Except for right now, when I clicked it a few times. I wasn't aware I was doing it until I saw Peterman's eyes move down from my optics to my mouth and then back.

"Yeah, well," he said, "we had a solution for it once, but that didn't work out."

"A solution for Thornton's insoluable problem?"

Peterman's face cracked into a grin as wide as the summer sky. "Thornton's problem? Hey, I like it, Sparks, I like it. But yeah, there was a way around it. It was a few years ago now—oh, I know, you don't remember, I got it—but listen, you and I helped each other out on a little problem."

"Thornton's or someone else's?"

"Little problem with the Ruskies, Sparks. And that guy in the wheelchair. Now he was something else." He waved his hands in the air like he could sculpt a guy in a wheelchair out of nothing but the summer breeze. "Anyway, we got that tidied away and actually it did you a favor. Turns out the Soviets had been working on something that wasn't entirely different to Thornton's insoluble problem and they'd got something together that worked, and pretty well too."

Peterman's eyes dropped to my chest. He nodded and sniffed and then he stepped forward and lifted one lapel of my trench coat. I didn't stop him, but I did take a half step back.

Peterman pulled his hands away like a man caught trying to lift a handbag from someone's grandmother.

"Hey, come on, we're friends, Sparks, remember? Oh no, sorry, you don't." He clicked his fingers in annoyance.

"Keep talking and maybe you can get back on my Christmas card list," I said.

Peterman grinned. "Now we're in business, Sparks! So listen, the Soviets had developed a memory cube, some kind of three-dimensional digital matrix I think, read by a fixed laser array. Anyway, I don't know the details. That was Ada's department."

"Ada?"

"You going to let me tell you about how we saved your life or not?"

"We?"

"Yeah, Sparks. We! Me and Ada and Eva."

"Eva?"

"Are you going to listen or not?"

I kept my mouth grille shut.

"Okay, so, we get this crystal and we install it in your chest. You know, to replace your memory tape. We had to make a new plate, of course. By the way your shirt keeps unbuttoning I guess you still have it."

I found the fingers of my right hand had moved up and were feeling the buttons of my shirt just underneath my tie. Sure enough, the third one down had come undone. I did it back up but it felt a little tight.

"So yeah," said Peterman, "we put the crystal in and everything's fine and now you don't have to forget anything."

"Except I don't have a digital crystal as a memory store," I said.

Peterman clicked his fingers again. "Right, Sparks, right! It was swapped out and the tape array was put back in. Ada called us back to help out. Seems the crystal wasn't working out, for some reason. A crying shame. For a while there I didn't need to tell you who won the Oscar for best actor in a leading role for three years straight every day."

I didn't say anything. Peterman frowned at me, then said, "The answer to that question is me, Sparks. Fresco Peterman!"

"You're telling me you're a movie star?" I said. I wasn't sure if he was telling the truth but then there was no reason for him to lie. Especially as we were old friends.

Apparently.

Peterman didn't look too happy. I thought maybe he had been waiting for me to congratulate him on his success rather than question his *bona fides* so I kept talking.

"Which explains," I said, "the scene at the BCFC. You use a different name on the membership list because you're a celebrity. But the club has had trouble with reporters finding out and trying to ambush its most famous member, which is why your club captain has a tendency to jump to conclusions when people or robots show up unannounced."

Peterman narrowed his eyes as he listened and he nodded his head like it was the first time he'd heard this theory expounded. Then he clicked his fingers and his smile turned back on all at the same time.

"Hey, who's the detective now, huh?"

"So you need to talk to me?" I asked.

"Right again, Sparks." Peterman made yet another flying visit to the interior of his sedan. This time he reached over the driver's side to the glove box. He pulled something out and pulled himself out of the car and he passed that something to me. I looked at it in his outstretched hand. He shook it at me. It was a book of some kind.

"What is it?" I asked, not lifting a finger to take it.

"Sparks, listen, you're killing me here, killing me! This is yours, you big hunk of scrap metal. You gave it to me to look after last night—remember, you took it out from under the spare wheel . . . oh, yeah, of course you don't remember. Well, look, you said it was important and that you'd want it back the next day, which was technically the same day, but let's not get into all that. It makes my head hurt."

"You should be so lucky," I said. My own headache was coming back. As I took the book from Peterman I adjusted the resistance in the motherboard system bus on my left side but it didn't make me feel any better.

I didn't know anything about what had gone down last night, but the fact that the book had been under the spare wheel rang a hell of an alarm right in the middle of my positronic brain. The book was clearly what Touch Daley had wanted me to find. Only he hadn't known I'd passed it on for safekeeping.

The book was a paperback novel. The cover was creased and it featured a guy in spacesuit cradling a woman in a chainmail bikini. They looked like they were on the moon except the rocks were pink and there was a green monster coming over the rim of a crater. The guy in the spacesuit had a ray gun in his free hand but it didn't look like it would do much against the impending danger.

I held the book in my hands and glanced up at Peterman. He had turned his face up to sun and seemed to be enjoying the great outdoors.

"You know a guy called Touch Daley?" I asked.

Peterman blinked and I wasn't sure it was because of the light in his eyes. He turned his head to face me.

"You remember Touch Daley?"

"Sure," I said, "because he paid me a visit this morning. He told me I was in danger and that I needed to check under the spare wheel."

Peterman whistled between his teeth. When he did that the breeze picked up like he had called it, but it was just a coincidence. I glanced up behind him and saw a few clouds gathering over the crest of the next hill ahead.

"Boy, they're moving fast now. Seventeen already. Phew. And he came to visit in person? Phew. Things are moving, Sparks, things are moving."

"Seventeen what?"

"Seventeen Touch Daleys. Last night—I mean, this morning—it was only sixteen and I thought we were ahead."

I didn't know what that meant. Seventeen Touch Daleys? As far as I knew—and this was from firsthand experience— Touch Daley was a human being and most often they only came in ones.

On the other hand, the Touch Daley who had visited me this morning was wearing a tight black trilby and I just happened to have another one just like it getting warm in the sun on the passenger seat of my car.

I didn't like where that particular train was headed.

I looked at Peterman. I saw he'd gone back to quiet contemplation as he leaned against the car, his lips moving as he looked at the dirt. I didn't want to interrupt so I returned my attention to the book—and what was inside it. Because while the book was old and well read, it wasn't what was printed on the pages that was interesting. Between a good deal of them were small sheets of folded yellow notepaper, tucked in so they didn't poke out the sides but enough to make the book swell so it didn't close properly.

I took out one of the sheets. It was written on in a thin gray pencil in a handwriting that was mine. It was just like the note that had brought me to Fresco Peterman at the BCFC.

The first page had some sparse notes about a club on the Sunset Strip and mentioned a woman called Honey. I pulled out another, and this one had a description of the replacement chest panel that Peterman knew about and a suggestion that I ask Ada about it.

I leafed through some more. There were names and places. Zeus Falzarano. Alfie Micklewhite. Emerson Ellis Building and Construction. The address for an Italian restaurant. I kept looking and I found Peterman's name, along with someone called Eva McLuckie—the Eva he had mentioned—and someone else called Charles David.

I flipped to the back and I found what I presumed was the most recent note. It had just one word on it— Esmerelda—and I could see the impression of the note before still embossed on the surface. I tilted the paper to catch the light and read the ghost of my own instruction, GO HERE INSTEAD, along with the address I now knew to be of the gym in Bay City.

I looked at Peterman. He was watching me now. I saw him watching and I closed the book and put it into the pocket of my coat.

"Thanks, I think."

"Anytime, Sparks, anytime. So, look, if seventeen made contact with you already, then things are moving, and moving fast."

"So you said," I said.

Peterman frowned again. "If they're moving that quickly then we don't have much time. I need to get back to town and get ready. You need to get back to your office and pretend nothing has happened, okay?"

"Ada isn't going to buy that," I said. "She sent me out on a job and I'm going to have some explaining to do if I haven't done it."

Peterman cocked his head. "What was the job?"

I fished inside my jacket for the ticker tape. I handed it over. Peterman peered at it.

"Just a name and an address," I said. "Specifically, your name. The address I don't know. Do you recognize it?"

Peterman nodded and then he laughed and that laugh kept on going as he handed the tape back to me.

"That Ada, she's a doll. Always one step ahead. She's good, Ray, very good. I'm sure Professor Thornton would be proud to see what she's become."

I wasn't entirely sure about that but I kept that particular thought to myself. As I stuffed the tape back into my pocket, Peterman nodded in my general direction.

"That address is my beach house—well, one of them. Ada wasn't sending you to kill me; she was sending you to *meet* me. Only we—you and me—decided on another rendezvous last night. There's more than a fair chance that house is being watched, and we don't know that Ada knows that."

If I could have raised an eyebrow I would have. Peterman seemed to sense it because he raised his hands again. "Hey, Sparks, it was your idea! And a good one too. You've got a nose for trouble, I'll give you that."

"So Ada knows about you—and us?"

"Everything, Ray. Everything."

Then the famous movie star cleared his throat and checked over his shoulder, but we were still alone and not a single car had come along the hill road since we'd stopped.

"Okay, Ray, okay, time to roll. I'll get into position. You go back to the office. Maybe, I don't know, make some more notes. You're going to have to wait, but I'm pretty sure things will get off the ground today. I'll be in touch."

With that he swung back into his car and he swung the car back onto the road and he was gone in a spit of gravel and a cloud of dust.

I stood and waited long enough for the dust to settle and then I stood and listened to the birds and the breeze in the trees. I could feel the paperback book in my pocket and it felt like it was made of four-inch armor plating.

Then I got back into my car and turned back onto the road and I followed it down the hill and all the while I wondered what I had gotten myself into this time.

No, not me.

Ada.

Because right now it felt like trouble was my business, and business was good.

11

I didn't go straight back to the office but it wasn't until I was back in town and cruising Sunset Boulevard that I decided to turn tail and go somewhere quieter to think. Maybe I decided the moment I passed a club on a corner where I had, according to my notes, met a girl called Honey. Maybe I had made the decision long before then.

I drove back into the hills. I didn't know where I was going but I got there anyway, winding up the hills and then down a narrow road that was mostly dirt until I slid the Buick through an old chicken-wire gate and into a small dusty lot behind the Hollywood sign. There had been a sign on the gate telling me to think twice about what I was doing, but the gate was open and the parking lot was empty and it seemed like a good spot for a little contemplation. There was a hut by the lot, a long rectangular thing with a green roof and a sign on the side that said it belonged to the

City of Los Angeles Department of Parks and Recreation.

When the car was off I rolled down the window and I reached into my pocket and I took out the book and I started reading the yellow sheets of notepad concealed within.

What they said was interesting but not illuminating. I read them through three times even though I remembered exactly what was on them after the first time. Part of me wanted to be sure, and rereading what I already knew gave me something to do while my para-neuristic calculators did an awful lot of complex math.

When I was done I sat and I looked out at the view from the hill until the sun went down and the moon came up and the lights on the Hollywood sign went on. I hadn't known the sign was illuminated. I thought it was just a sign. It ran in sequence, first the **HOLLY** flashing white and then the **WOOD** flashing white and then the whole **HOLLYWOOD** blazing three more times. It must have been hell on house prices for those unlucky enough to live on the twisting streets just below.

While I sat there I kept expecting the telephone by my elbow to ring but it never did and that was fine. Ada knew I was out on a job and I could look after myself. In fact, according to my new—or old—friend Fresco Peterman, Ada knew exactly what I was doing today.

After a few more hours of smelling the cooling desert air and listening to coyotes awaken as the light died I went back into the book, to the last note. It had been written after my past self had given my future self the instruction to meet Peterman, but I had no idea what it meant and Peterman hadn't said anything. I should have asked him, but I'd had other things on my circuits.

Esmerelda.

I wondered who that was. She wasn't mentioned elsewhere in the notes. She must have been important to get a page all to herself.

I put the note back into the book and checked my watch. It was late. I'd wasted a whole lot of time, which was something Peterman said we were short on. But he also said Ada was in on this grand plan so I figured she would have called if things were moving.

But it was still time to go. I put the book in my pocket and I started the car. Then I turned the car off and I got out and I went around to the trunk and I opened it and I got the floor out and I put the book back under the spare wheel.

Then I got back in behind the wheel and I headed back to the office.

It was later still by the time I got back to town but that didn't mean it was any quieter. According to my permanent store, New York was the city that never sleeps, but I was pretty sure the sentiment could be applied to that other town on the opposite coast.

People were about and some were in cars and some were on foot. Lights blazed and flashed and I drove on.

And as I got closer to the office I saw other lights that blazed and flashed. Blue and red, moving and strobing and sweeping the intersection of Cahuenga and Hollywood, on the corner of which sat the building that housed the Electromatic Detective Agency. The lights did a good job of illuminating the building too, almost to the floor where Ada sat.

I counted a half dozen police cars arranged around

the intersection, another three lined up nose to tail at the curb outside the building's main door, and another parked at an angle on the ramp that led to the parking garage, blocking access.

I kept on driving and shot through the intersection at a reasonable speed. I kept going a block and then I looped around and came back down a parallel street and then blew back through the intersection again. That might have been a mistake but none of the cops appeared to be on the lookout for my vehicle. I went on another block and then pulled over and stopped the car and waited. Then I looked in the rearview and turned around as best I could in the driver's seat to get a better look.

The office building was surrounded, as much as a building that sat on a corner could be said to be surrounded. There were more cops now out on the sidewalk and some of them were herding what pedestrians there were to the other side of the street. Nobody paid me any attention, which made me think this had nothing to do with the Electromatic Detective Agency. The building was not at full occupancy but there were plenty of other tenants.

That idea went out the window when I saw a tall man in a black suit walk out of the building, followed by two others with identical taste in clothing. Those two already had their black hats in place but the tall guy at the front was holding his in front of him, which came in pretty handy as he started waving it at the cops parked at the curb.

Touch Daley must have had a way with words because those cops jumped up like their asses were on fire and they moved the three cars in a short convoy farther down the street. Daley and his twin buddies stood talking for a little while longer out on the sidewalk and then three big black vans came around the intersection and pulled up in the space left by the police cruisers. Their doors opened and more men in black suits got out and then Touch Daley led the whole lot back into the building.

So yes, they were here for me.

Or for Ada.

I thought about the computer room behind the office. I thought about the secret room out on the other side, where all my memory tapes were stored. A complete record, chronological, catalogued, of all my crimes. I had no idea how many tapes were in there. Truth be told I had no idea how long I'd been doing this job. Ada had reprogrammed me, I knew that, but exactly when was lost in the electric fog of my life.

Touch Daley had visited this morning to give me a warning—about his own raid on the office? He'd said that trouble was coming and Fresco Peterman had agreed. Was this the trouble? Did Peterman know the raid was coming? And if Peterman knew, what about Ada?

Nothing added up. All I knew is that trouble had arrived and there didn't seem to be a whole lot I could do about it.

I watched the cops as they milled around. The black vans were unoccupied and while it was hard to see from my vantage point it looked like their loading doors were standing open. The men in black hadn't come back out of the building. Several of the office windows were lit and that included one of the windows in the agency office, but there was no movement to be seen and nothing changed as I sat and watched. I tried a few optical filters, from ultraviolet to infrared, and while some of them worked quite well to brighten the scene, the flashing lights of the police cruisers quickly turned everything into shapeless flares. I tried infraviolet and ultrared but all that did was throw magenta spots everywhere and I cut the feed before my anti-neutron collector comb got too hot.

I watched some more and nothing happened. Those cops on the street were collecting a nice piece of overtime for shooting nothing but the breeze.

I turned back around in my seat. The street ahead was now devoid of traffic and farther on at the next intersection the traffic lights flashed orange as they swung above the roadway. I'd been sitting here a long time.

I looked down at the telephone between the two front seats. I picked it up. I dialed the office. If the agency was full of cops and Touch Daley and his friends then maybe they were all sitting around my desk and standing around the room, smoking in silence, staring at the telephone, waiting for it to ring, Ada in custody, as much as you could arrest a room, but refusing to cooperate, and everyone waiting for the last robot in the world to call in.

I knew how it would go. They'd pick up. They'd want to keep me talking, keep the line open while their boffins pored over their equipment, trying to get a fix on where I was. They'd make promises, maybe threats, maybe tell me it was no good and that I should give myself up before my memory tape ran out.

My logic gates clicked and got warm as I thought about all the ways in which this telephone call was the wrong thing to do but I was going to do it anyway. The telephone rang in my ear and to take my processor off things I counted the rings.

I got to twenty-five and it was still going. I rolled down

the window with my free hand and I listened to the sleeping city but even with my audio receptors at full power and filtering for all they were worth—which was several million taxpayer dollars—I was too far away from the office and I couldn't hear a telephone ringing on the inside of it if my life depended on it.

Which I very much thought it might.

After forty-two rings I put the telephone down and then I sat and I waited and I did nothing but computate and calculate.

The telephone hadn't been answered, which meant either Ada wasn't answering it deliberately or she was being prevented from answering it—by, say, being disconnected from the line. That was the worst-case scenario but if there was ever a time to brace for impact then it was right about now.

I checked the time. It was late and my memory tape was not going to last forever. Far from it. And when it ran out . . .

Well, I didn't like to think what would happen when it ran out. I wished that Fresco Peterman hadn't told me about the digital crystal I'd once had installed because, problems or not, not having to worry about my memory getting full sounded real swell.

I had no choice. I had to find out just what this world of trouble was that I'd driven myself into. I couldn't solve a problem without knowing what it was.

I opened the driver's door and I got out and I closed it with a click that was firm and quiet and yet seemed to echo like a gunshot around the dead street. But I had no time to pause and wait and look and listen. The cops hadn't noticed my car but they might just notice a robot dawdling on the sidewalk.

Luckily I knew the area and I knew the streets within it. It was all on my permanent store. I could approach the building around the back, where there was an alley that stretched between the office block and the brown brick building next door. The window in the back office looked out over this alley. That alley had a fire escape that went up and a fire door or two that went inside. I knew the building, including parts of it that didn't appear on any blueprints filed down at city hall. There was a chance I could get in and take a look and maybe not get caught.

A slim one, but it seemed the night for it.

I turned and hit the sidewalk and headed east, away from the building and the cop cars and their lights. All I had to do was get to the next intersection and take a left and then another left and then I could get through a backstreet and I could be in the alley.

I had a whole half hour to go before my memory tape ran out. As I walked at a pace that was fairly brisk toward the intersection I told myself that that was all the time in the world.

And it was. Quite literally.

I kept walking. I passed closed stores and the empty street. The stores rounded the corner and so did the sidewalk. The intersection was dead and lit by the slowly flashing lights of the traffic signs swinging from their cables above. There was a telephone booth on the corner.

That was when the telephone inside began to ring.

Twenty-eight minutes and thirty-two seconds until the end of the world.

Time enough for a chat.

I opened the door of the telephone booth and I reached

inside and I answered the telephone. I didn't bother to squeeze all the way into the booth. There was nobody around to see or hear. I stood on the sidewalk with the stiff metal cable of the telephone snaking out through the door and as I put the receiver to the side of my head I watched the lights of the police cruisers far away mix with the lights of the sleeping traffic lights a good deal closer.

There was a click, and a rush of white noise. Somewhere in that I thought I heard the sound of someone taking a long hard drag on a cigarette, the kind of drag you take after a long hard day at the office before you kick off your shoes and start looking for some liquid refreshment, preferably the kind that comes in a very small glass with a lot of ice.

And maybe I heard that ice clinking too, somewhere. But if I did it was gone as soon as I realized it. Maybe it was just my imagination.

"Ada?"

"Ray, hi," said Ada. "Listen, you wouldn't believe the kind of day I've had."

12

I stepped closer to the telephone booth. The street was still empty but I had the sudden urge for a little more privacy and with the door closed behind me I felt just a little bit better.

I put all my other questions to one side. I had suspicions and I had theories and I had questions like you wouldn't believe, but they could wait, because there was just one thing on my mind now and I was well aware of the consequences.

I shifted my weight and I checked my watch and I brought the telephone mouthpiece up to my grille.

"Ada, I have twenty-seven minutes flat before my memory tape runs out. You need to tell me what's happening and you need to tell me now."

There was the sound of the cigarette being used for its singular purpose.

"Well, I'll have to admit, things are not going entirely how I would like them."

"Ada!"

"Look, they came for us, Ray, okay?"

"Who's they?"

"The Department of Robot Labor. I tried to reach you but nobody picked up."

"I was a little occupied, Ada. I was having a chat with a certain Fresco Peterman. He had quite a story to tell."

"Good, you made contact. So you should be filled in."

I sighed. The sound rattled the glass of the telephone booth. "I know even less about the state of the world than I did when I got up this morning. All he said was that we three musketeers were cooking something up, and that we all knew what it was except old Raymondo here kept losing track. He said I should go back to the office and that we would be in touch but neither of those things seems very likely anymore, do they?"

"Right on all counts, chief," said Ada. "Things moved faster than we thought."

"That's what he said."

Ada laughed. One loop, full and throaty and with the rasp of a pack-a-day smoker.

"What do I do, Ada? The countdown clock is running and I'm not sure I want to find out what happens when it gets to zero."

"Okay, let me see what I can do."

"You'll forgive me if that doesn't fill me with confidence. Twenty-five minutes, Ada."

The roar of static filled the airwaves and buried somewhere within the noise was the sound of the fast hand of a stopwatch.

"Ada?"

"Okay, where are you?"

I looked around and gave my location, but I wasn't sure how that was going to help and I said as much. Then I switched the telephone's earpiece to the other side of my head and asked a very particular question that was burning a hole through my tertiary oscillator.

"Where are *you*, Ada? I called before but you didn't connect. If Daley and his boys are in the office—"

"Don't you worry your pretty little head about that, Ray. Momma can look after herself."

I turned and looked over my shoulder. I opened the door of the telephone booth. I listened to the night. I looked around some more.

And then I imagined the office full of cops and their smoke and their sweat and Touch Daley leaning over one of his black-suited boys as they twisted dials and made notes and passed a set of well-used federal-issue headphones up to his boss. Were they listening in now, getting a trace, finding out I was just down the street?

Hell, they didn't have to do a trace. I'd just told Ada right where I was.

I pulled myself back into the booth and pulled the door closed with a loud snap and then I pulled the telephone hand piece closer to the grille of my mouth. "Are they listening now? Did they make you call? What have they forced you to do, Ada?"

Ada laughed. Two full loops this time. Then she smoked and laughed some more.

"Twenty minutes. I don't like the joke," I said.

"Oh, Ray, sorry, sorry," said Ada. "Listen. You can trust me. When have I ever let you down?"

I thought back to my notes, hidden under the spare wheel, in the trunk of my car, parked down the street. Right where Daley and his boys could find it if they just happened to glance in that direction.

"I'm not sure I can rightly answer that question, Ada."

"Raymondo, you're a doll. But listen, and listen good. Things are moving fast but that just means we have to move faster. I'm going to make a couple calls and then—"

There was a click inside my head and then silence and then after a few moments the dial tone rang like a bell in my audio receptor and kept on going until the line clicked again and another voice spoke.

"Operator?"

I slammed the telephone home and I closed the door of the booth behind me. What was Ada doing? I had eighteen minutes and twenty-two seconds left and I had the feeling I was going to spend most of that wondering just what the hell was going on.

I had no choice. If this was the end of my career then I was going to go out fighting. Eighteen minutes.

Time enough to get to the office and see just what was going on for myself and to hell with the consequences.

13

I made it down the street and around to the side alley that ran parallel to my office building with fifteen minutes to spare.

The alley was dark and I was the only thing moving in it. I walked along it and as I did I looked up. There were a lot of windows that looked out onto the alley and some of them were lit. I counted the requisite number up and across and found what was the window in the computer room. The light was on there too and as I stood and looked up I saw shapes moving. I didn't know how many people were in there but I had a theory or two about what they were doing.

And now I knew who they were: agents from the Department of Robot Labor. That made a kind of sense, as they were the federal agency responsible for the great robot revolution in the first place, with Professor Thornton as their chief scientific advisor and architect of the national robotics project. From Thornton's genius for electronic invention had come designs and those designs were turned into technology that allowed the production of hundreds— thousands, tens of thousands—of mechanical people, from factories all over the country. There were dumb robots and there were smart ones, and there were fast ones and slow ones, strong ones and those built for more delicate tasks. A good deal of them were designed for function over form, but most were built to look like people and sound like people. At least, that was the idea. The theory behind this was that people were going to like working alongside machines that walked and talked like they did, and that they'd feel better with these machine men and women and gender-unspecified doing all the kinds of jobs that people didn't want to do or only did because there was nothing better available, whether it was taking out the trash or directing traffic or packing your brown paper bags at the supermarket and taking the groceries out to the car or staying at home and cutting the grass and trimming the hedges or running oil rigs or servicing airplanes or running the accounts at the town council. Hell, some people even thought that maybe, just maybe, the human part of the population would make friends with the electronic part.

The problem became apparent fairly quickly and it was fairly serious, but this was a federal program that a lot of people had taken a lot of time and money to plan and that was taking an even larger amount of money to start, so it wasn't going to be stopped. Not until it was almost too late.

Because it turned out that people didn't like machines that looked and sounded like them. And with all the jobs that were considered menial taken by machines, a great slice of the newly freed people found that the so-called leisure time the government had promised also went by another name: chronic unemployment. It turned out that to enjoy a life without responsibility you still needed a little thing called money, and those who had money before the robots came along—and that included a fair proportion of old men in the nation's capital who were very keenly pushing the robot revolution along—still had it when the robots arrived so that problem was never anticipated.

At least that's what my permanent store said. To me that sounded like a less than ideal way to run a government and like those old men with money needed to learn a lesson or two about how the world really worked, but I imagined that stranger things had happened and in the grand scheme of the universe this was probably just par for the course.

So while robots helped children cross the street outside their school and some of them even taught chemistry to the seniors, there was now a not inconsiderable proportion of the population without work and without the means to support itself. The so-called robot revolution had sliced like a knife right through the middle of society, damaging the country in ways that nobody could really comprehend, not even those with some clue as to what was going on.

And all that before the *other* problem came up. They had a name for that one, too.

Robophobia.

Nobody knew or even suspected it existed, but it was there all right, a latent, primal fear, buried deep in the collective psyche. Put simply, it was a fear of robots—or at least that is how it manifested. A fear, not of the unlike, but of the almost-but-not-quite like. Not everyone had it and for most who did the doctor could give you something along with your usual prescription for tranquilizers.

But some people got it and got it bad, and it did terrible things and then somebody called it an epidemic and they may even have said it on the TV news and that led to protests and protests led to violence and a lot of other things appearing on the TV news that made people weep in the small hours. The country nearly tore itself apart and nearly lost a president in the process.

The federal robot program was canceled. Every robot was recalled. The entire matter was consigned to history, and, according to my permanent store, it became something of a taboo subject to discuss.

I was aware of all this, each day. I had the whole history of the robot program in my permanent store. Thornton had put it there. I was the last robot in the world, after all, and he knew right from the start that I was going to encounter all kinds of reactions when people saw me walking down the sidewalk. Forewarned was forearmed, the saying went, and I knew that because it was also in my permanent store. A personal piece of advice from my creator.

But there was something else, and as I watched the shapes move in the window of the office high above, that something bothered me more than a little. Because the end of the robot program also meant the end of the Department of Robot Labor. It was closed down along with my mechanical brethren and some important people were made to resign, some even in public, and everyone else got reassigned and nobody spoke of it again.

So quite what the defunct department was doing here

now, in my office, in the computer room, most likely in my memory tape archive, was a question that came to mind readily enough.

Thirteen minutes.

I slipped down the alley. I was hidden in the darkness, and the forever-moving lights of all the cop cars out on the main street were doing me a favor because none of the light shone directly into the alley and to anyone out on the sidewalk the alley would just be one big black empty nothing.

I pulled myself against the brown brick and I cast an optic over the scene.

Something started to happen.

The cops still stood around with folded arms and they'd been there long enough for me to hope someone had gone to get coffee and donuts. There were none of Daley's agents around, but the three black vans were still parked at the curb with enough room between each for their rear doors to be swung wide open.

Two black-suited agents, each with a clipboard in his hands, jumped out of two of the vans. They stood by the back doors of their vehicles and looked at the building.

At almost the same time, the main building doors slammed open and a stream of agents emerged. Some were carrying objects, either solo or with the help of a colleague. Yet more were wheeling larger items out with handcarts. The procession made their way to the vans and the process of loading began while the ones with the clipboards began making notes.

It was a smooth operation, the precious cargo coming out of the building and disappearing into the vehicles and the agents swinging around and heading back inside for the next load.

And precious was the right way to describe what they were moving. There were consoles and control boards. There were boxes that were studded with lights on the front and trailed wires from the rear. Some of the larger components on the dollies included mainframe computers and data storage banks, each the size of a household refrigerator.

They were all from the computer room. All parts of Ada, broken down into her individual, modular components. She'd always been federal property and the government had finally come to collect it back. That explained why our call had been cut. They had literally pulled the plug.

And then there were the cardboard boxes. They were twelve inches square and four inches high and the agents carried them in stacks balanced against their chests. The boxes were sealed with yellow tape and even though I couldn't see them I knew they had labels on the lids that were filled in with neat handwriting in black ink. My handwriting.

The boxes contained my memory tapes—the master ones, bigger reels that could hold a lot more than twenty-four hours, the archive compiled from the small micro-reel tape that wound on in my chest and had, at the moment, just eight minutes of space left.

I backed away from the alley entrance and I sank into the shadows. I turned down the faint glow of my optics and I pulled down the brim of my hat and then I wondered what I was doing because none of it mattered. In seven minutes and thirty seconds the life and times of Raymond Electromatic would come to an end and the world really would be without robots. I guessed that when my systems ground to a halt and I toppled over in the alley everyone out on the street would hear and when they found me they'd have the complete set.

That was when the flare of a match appeared at the far end of the alleyway. I watched as the flame vanished and was replaced by a glowing red pinpoint of light as someone took a long, hard pull on a cigarette.

I took a step forward. I had six minutes left.

"Peterman?"

There was no sound from the smoker. I took another step.

"Ada?"

This got a reaction. It was a laugh, and I had heard the voice it belonged to just this morning, but it was male and it wasn't Peterman's.

I flipped my optics to infrared and there he was. A tall man with a strong nose and a square jaw and thin lips and the short stiff rim of a black hat pulled low.

Five minutes and forty seconds and the last person I wanted to meet in a dark alley was federal agent Touch Daley.

The cigarette flared. I switched my optics back to regular vision and I watched as the glowing red nub floated down in the darkness as Daley let his hand hang by his side.

"Mr. Electromatic," he said. "Funny meeting you here."

"Yeah, it's a real scream," I said. "Give me five minutes and eleven seconds and I can give you a whole routine."

Agent Daley stepped toward me and into a dull glowing cone of light cast from the windows above us. The cigarette burned between the fingers of his left hand but my attention was drawn to the other, which was holding a gun.

At least, I thought that's what it was. It was large and bulbous, like a glass sculpture the shape of a large pine cone filled with electronic circuitry and wires. The thing didn't have a barrel as such, just a slightly pointed end. That end was pointed right at me.

I held up my hands. I wasn't surrendering to the agent. I was surrendering to fate. I was out of time. It was all over. I had a few minutes of life left and this particular chapter of Los Angeles history was going to come to an ignoble end in a dark alley.

I tried to think of some last words but nothing in particular came to mind.

"I guess you got what you wanted," I said. It was better than nothing and it seemed to fit.

Special Agent Daley nodded and smoked and nodded again. The gun stayed where it was. He didn't speak. I measured the wattage across the positive and negative terminals of my bidirectional signal amplifier and found it was running a little high.

How disappointing.

Then Touch Daley said, "I guess I did," and then he lifted the gun and squeezed the trigger and the Hollywood night was filled with blue and purple dancing stars and the sound of the ocean crashing on rocks far away.

14

I woke up. I turned my optics on. The image was ****** ERROR 66 ****** monochrome and cast in green and white **!!PROGRAM BREAK!!** and it was hazy at the edges, like I was looking at the world through a thin fabric.

Light moved. I could see that much. It was dark and it was green and maybe I was looking at the ceiling of a room or maybe I wasn't because a moment later my audio receptors cut in and I heard the roar of the ocean again and then the world shook and I bumped the back of my head against something hard and metal.

I wanted to say something along the lines of "ouch," even though I didn't feel pain in the way that people felt pain, only an approximation of pain, a computerized simulation of the neural impulses that were associated with pain inside the brain of my creator, Professor Thornton, and they were associated with pain inside my own positronic central computation core because Thornton had imprinted it with the template of his own mind.

All of which meant that when Professor Thornton hit his head and it hurt he tended to say "ouch" before rubbing the back of his skull and frowning at the world before him.

I tried to rub the back of my own skull but my arms wouldn't move. The green world around me got a great deal darker the more I tried to move and

And

And then

```
!!PROGRAM BREAK!!
**** ERROR 66 ****
```

And then

```
**** ERROR 66 ****
              **** ERROR 66 ****
                             **** ERROR 66 ****
```

And then

```
!!PROGRAM BREAK!! **** ERROR 66 **** SYSTEM
RESTART IN 5 . . .
                    4 . . .
                    3 . . .
                    2 . . .
                    1 . . .
```

And then I woke up and it was another beautiful day in Hollywood, California. Just like it always was, each and every morning when I woke in my alcove and the world was born anew.

Something was different, though. I didn't know how I knew it but I did. Whatever had been programmed on my permanent store about mornings in Hollywood, California, was enough to tell me that they weren't dark and green and fuzzy at the edges and they didn't smell of gasoline and dust and sweat and something else, something sharp and tangy and almost floral but also a little bit chemical.

I wasn't standing in my alcove. I was lying on the floor. There was a thin carpet and there was molded metal underneath and it shook a little. The room I was in was moving. Somewhere I heard an engine. Somewhere else I heard someone talking.

No, two people. Two men.

A shape moved in front of my optics. It was a greenish shadow against a greenish light and greenish static crawled around it. I could see a mouth moving and the shape—the man's head—got closer to my face and I could smell that smell again. It was aftershave. Something familiar. Maybe Thornton had worn aftershave just like it.

And then the shadow moved away and then

```
**** ERROR 66 ****
```

And then

```
**** ERROR 66 ****
                **** ERROR 66 ****
                            **** ERROR 66 ****
```

And then

```
!!PROGRAM BREAK!! **** ERROR 66 **** SYSTEM
RESTART IN 5 . . .
                    4 . . .
                    3 . . .
                    2 . . .
                    1 . . .
```

I woke up and it was another beautiful—

It was green and hazy and—

Shadows moved and as they moved they broke into more shadows and—

Someone spoke. A man. Wearing after

`!!PROGRAM BREAK!!`

shave and talking to someone else and

`**** ERROR 66 ****`

then and

`**** ERROR 66 ****`

then and

`**** ERROR 66 ****`

then and

`**** SYSTEM RESTART IN 5 . . .`

I was out of memory tape. I could feel it in my chest, the

`4 . . .`

small reel hitting the end and the mechanism rewinding, not

`3 . . .`

much, just a few minutes

`2 . . .`

and the system instigating an emergency restart to allow the tape

`1 . . .`

to record over itself and then
And then
      And then
            And then

And then I woke up and it was another beautiful day in Hollywood, California. Just like it always was, each and every morning when I woke in my alcove and the world was born anew.

Something was different though. I didn't know how I knew it but I did.

```
**** SYSTEM RESTART IN 5 . . .
                   4 . . .
                   3 . . .
                   2 . . .
                   1 . . .
```

I woke up and someone was speaking.

```
**** SYSTEM RESTART SUCCESSFUL END LOOP END
****
```

The world was a green haze but I concentrated like my life depended on it and I thought perhaps this time it really did. The green world turned into a black and white world but this one was a little sharper around the edges.

I was in the back of a van. I was lying on the floor. The van was moving but I wasn't. There were two men with me. One was wearing a hat and the other one wasn't.

The man without the hat was not quite young but he was very good looking and he had far-away eyes. His hair glistened with tonic and curved back from his forehead in an apparently immobile arc. He was wearing a jacket made out of a patterned fabric that made red glittery sparks at the edges of my vision. It was so dazzling you could have camouflaged a battleship with it.

I adjusted my optics and focused on his companion. He was older and also a handsome fellow but his looks were sharp and severe and he looked pretty angry about something. My guess was that he looked angry about something nearly all of the time. He was wearing a black suit and his hat was black and I could see the hair underneath that hat was also black. He had a theme going and I thought, good for him.

For a moment I thought I recognized them both and two words rattled up and down my logic gates but they couldn't have been their names because people weren't called names like that. And then my vision went from black and white to green and nothing and I felt something very strange happen behind the panel on my chest as the memory tape once more reached the end and began to wind back and then

```
!!PROGRAM BREAK!!
```

aftershave and talking to someone else and

```
**** ERROR 66 ****
```

I also wasn't standing in my alcove and

```
**** ERROR 66 ****
```

it was another beautiful day in Hollywood, California, and

```
**** ERROR 66 ****
```

and

```
**** SYSTEM RESTART IN 5 . . .
                        4 . . .
```

and that was when

```
                     3 . . .
```

I knew

```
                     2 . . .
```

that I was in a whole world of trouble

```
                     1 . . .
```

15

I woke up and it was another beautiful day in Hollywood, California. I opened my optics and adjusted the focus and stared at the window opposite my alcove. Across the street was a building made of rough brown bricks that caught the morning sun and cast little shadows worthy of the lunar landscape.

Except right now I couldn't see the brown brick building. The sun hadn't come up yet and the window in front of me was just a flat black screen.

I stepped forward and I stumbled. Something else wasn't right and I knew that too, even though my relativity comparator was screaming blue murder in my audio receptors that I shouldn't know a damned thing about it.

There was supposed to be a little two-inch step down from my alcove and I had stumbled because I had been expecting the step but my feet found nothing but a flat floor

ADAM CHRISTOPHER

beneath them. I reached for the cable coming out of my chest that connected me to Ada's mainframe but I couldn't twist the chunky plastic plug to release myself on account of there was no chunky plug. The cable was thin and without any particular weight, not like the fat corrugated cable like something from a plumber's surplus store that should have been there. I knew about the cable because it was on my permanent store, alongside instructions about how to plug it in and what happened when I did.

The room was still as black as a coal cellar with a blown lightbulb. I let go of the thin cable and I turned up my optics and I looked down. The cable was a thick plastic flex that split into two separate lines about twelve inches or so from a plug in my chest that was a good deal smaller than the one that was supposed to be plugged in. I felt along the cable, but it didn't tell me anything I didn't already know.

It wasn't my cable, and I wasn't standing in my alcove, and I sure as hell wasn't in the office.

I took another step and I turned my optics up and then I switched on the infrared and my world turned green but at least it was a bright green.

I was standing in a small room with concrete block walls and the flat black window in front me was actually a flat black wall. Beside me was a silver wheeled trolley with some kind of gadget on it. The gadget was boxlike and about the size of a good-sized treasure chest. It had an angled front, where there was a tape running between two reels that were each ten inches in diameter. The tape had only just started feeding from the left to the right and it moved slowly. There were some buttons underneath the reels and some dials above them and as I moved my fingers

112

over the device I saw the dials move. I lifted my hand and I flexed the fingers and then I did the same with my other hand. The dials flickered when I moved and they didn't when I didn't.

I reached for the flex plugged into my chest compartment and pulled it up until it got tight. I saw then that the twin plugs on the other end were connected to the back of the tape machine. There was no other cabling and the machine was not connected to anything else in the room. I checked an internal electrical map and confirmed what I thought. I was powering the machine with a standard voltage equivalent to wall socket power alongside the lower voltage being transmitted along the second cable. That one was a data cable and not a particularly high capacity one, but it was doing the job. The memory tape in my chest was still in place but it wasn't moving.

Someone had hooked me up to a bypass. I thought that was pretty clever and I hoped to meet whoever had done it to congratulate them on their skill and expertise and then grab them by the neck and apply pressure until they told me where the hell I was.

I pushed the trolley. It moved silently on big, well-oiled wheels that had thick rubber tires. That was a help. I was pretty well oiled myself so it didn't seem like moving around was going to be a problem. I checked the voltage again and then I checked the drain on my atomic battery. The draw was higher than standard and that was to be expected but I could set my turbines to *speed* and it wouldn't make much difference. It was my memory that was the time constraint, not my power supply.

The fact that I was hooked up to a memory bypass gave

me all kinds of bad ideas, nearly all of which were variations on the fact that the tape in my chest had come to the end of its twenty-four-hour capacity. Which meant I hadn't got back to the office in time and I certainly wasn't there now.

Either I hadn't been able to get home—or had been prevented from getting there—or there was no longer a home to go to.

I didn't like either of those ideas at all but the latter gave my condenser coil a fresh coating of frost. Because if Ada had been compromised and there was no office to plug myself into then the bypass tape recorder on the silver trolley was anything but a permanent solution.

I looked around the room again but it hadn't changed any. Small, rectangular, empty. Some kind of storage cupboard. Maybe you'd call it a room if you were in a generous mood.

I wasn't.

With one hand I looped up my cables and stowed the loop around one end of the trolley and then I pushed the trolley to the door. The door was big and heavy and it was locked and the lock was big and heavy. I was in some kind of industrial building, a factory or a warehouse or a depot.

Fortunately I was bigger and heavier than either the lock or the door so I made short work of the former with as little sound as possible and then I stepped through the latter and drew it shut again behind me. From the outside the lock and handle looked intact so I thought that might buy me some time.

I glanced at the tape recorder. The dials twitched. The tape had moved on more than I liked.

The corridor was more concrete and it was still dark and I couldn't hear anything in particular. I looked left and right. I switched my optics back to visible light and went through a few more filters and I adjusted the gain but that didn't tell me anything so I switched back to infrared and once I'd made a couple more adjustments to the picture I picked a direction and took it with my little trolley rolling in front of me.

16

I walked down one corridor and then another and there was nothing much of interest in either. I didn't know where I was and I was pretty keen to find out and I was ready to do some of that old-fashioned detective work to do so but no clues were offering themselves up. What I needed was either the front door or a telephone. Hell, even the back door. Maybe I'd even locate a person or two I could ask a couple of questions. Before or after I had cracked their heads, I hadn't yet decided.

I kept going. More concrete corridors. More darkness. More silence. Then I turned a corner and came to a door. It was smaller and far less substantial than the one I had just gotten past but like that one and every other surface in this building it was painted a dull military gray. I even switched my optics back to visible light to check. When I switched back to infrared the handle flared in my filters and when I looked away to let them compensate I was left with a trail like a comet in the middle of my vision.

I tried the door. It was unlocked. I took that to be a promising development in the mystery and what else I took to be promising was the sound of a telephone ringing. It came from behind the very door I was staring at so I wasted no time in opening it.

Maybe Ada wasn't compromised. Maybe she was fine and the office was where it should be.

Which meant it was me who had been compromised. I'd been grabbed and dumped here. My memory tape had run out and my captors had come up with the bypass to keep me going just long enough for . . . well, for whatever they wanted me for.

Beyond the door was a square room with a low ceiling and the room was filled with boxes and dust and the sound of the telephone's bell. As I looked around something flashed and flared in my optics bright enough for me to take a step back into the hallway and take pause. I had to cycle through a few more filters and adjust the voltage for the afterimage to clear and when it did I stepped back inside and I saw that I was facing a wall lined with mirrors set above some kind of bench.

The telephone was ringing in the corner and when I got to it I saw it was covered in as much dust as the rest of the place. If I didn't know better, I would have said I'd just walked into the dressing room of a theater. That didn't do much to narrow my location down. Los Angeles was a big town and there were probably quite a number of joints like this one.

But it was a start.

I picked up the phone and there was a click in my audio receptor and for a second I heard the ocean, far away. Then it was gone and replaced with a rhythmic ticking, like there was an electrical outlet shorting somewhere close and the short was filling the air with radio noise.

"Hello?" I said. The call had to be for me. Somehow Ada knew where I was at just the right moment. It was a gift, I had to give her that.

The line just ticked in my ear. I spoke again but I got no reply, but the line didn't disconnect either. I waited and I counted the ticks, and I measured the rhythm of them. It was regular, sure, but if there was a coded message coming through then I wasn't getting it.

"Ada, is that you?"

Nothing but a hiss and a roar and a tick, tick, tick.

I drew the mouthpiece close to my grille.

"Ada, if that's you, then listen, I'm in trouble. I don't have much of a clue where I am and I think my memory tape has run out."

Tick, tick, tick.

"Ada?"

If silence could be said to be deafening then this one was breaking all kinds of city noise-control statutes.

"Ada, are you there? Do you know what's going on? Do you know where I am?"

Tick, tick, tick.

And then:

"Ray?"

Maybe the voice was in my head—scratch that, it *was* in my head, because that's how we talked to each other, by coded signal buried in the voltage coming through the telephone. The actual line connection was merely an accessory to the crime, a little trick that meant we couldn't be bugged because if anyone planted a microphone or tapped the line all they'd hear was the raw cry of the ever-expanding universe.

"Earth to Raymondo. Come in, Ray," said the voice. And then, "Hey, chief, you in there or what?"

I paused. I adjusted my grip on the telephone. I even switched it around to my other audio receptor just in case it would make a difference.

Because something wasn't right about the call.

I told myself to listen to the voice that wasn't in my head, that right now was real and alive and coming down the telephone line, vibrating in the earpiece, making an actual sound like it was a real phone call from someone I knew didn't exist outside a bunch of electric currents and fast-acting microswitches.

"Ada, is that you?"

The telephone continued to tick in the background and her voice was faint but unmistakable. As was her laugh. I listened and tried to count the loops but there were none.

If I didn't know any better, I would have said I was talking to somebody.

"What do you mean, 'Ada, is that you?'? Tell me, chief, who else would be calling you in the middle of the afternoon?" She paused. "Say, you haven't got someone else on the side, have you? Someone you're doing other jobs with? Actually, don't answer that one, not today. Things are difficult enough as it is without going through all that right now."

I gripped the telephone receiver hard enough for the plastic to crack. I wasn't sure Ada heard it against all the other competition on the line.

"Listen, Ada, what's going on? I'm not at the office. I woke up in some kind of storeroom. I don't know where I am yet. Might be some kind of old theater, but I need to keep looking. Preferably for the way out."

"Well, lucky I called, right? Don't tell me you thought I wouldn't? Raymondo, have a little faith!"

I turned around and let the telephone cord curl around me. I'd left the door of the dressing room open. I said "hold on," and I said it quietly as I picked up the telephone and moved to the door and moved to close it. Then I paused and I stepped out in the corridor. The telephone wouldn't come with me so I held it at an arm's length as I looked to the left and the right.

There. A sound. A door closing. Distance and direction were hard to judge, the way every little noise bounced around the concrete walls. The door had a swoosh, like it was closing against a cushion of air. I listened a moment. I turned my audio receptors up and then I turned them up some more.

Footsteps. A good pace, too, and while they were a long way away their owner wasn't making any kind of effort to be quiet. As I listened the footsteps got louder and by louder I assumed closer.

I stepped back into the dressing room and I pushed the door closed. It clicked shut, but when I looked down at the handle I saw there was a keyhole but no key.

I moved back to my trolley and I lifted the telephone again.

"We're okay," I said. "Someone might be coming. Listen, do you know where I am? I'm low on memory and—"

"Yes, Ray, I know," said Ada. "Now, you listen to me. I don't have much time."

"*You* don't have much time?" I glanced down at the tape recorder. "I'm out of memory and have been hooked up to some kind of, I don't know, a bypass. An external tape backup."

"That's great, Ray," said Ada. "Perfect."

I pursed my lips. On the inside, anyway. I found I liked the way it felt. Helped me to think. "You and I need to have a little talk about what you think is 'perfect' and what really isn't."

"It'll have to wait, chief. This is not a secure line. Someone could be listening."

"You got a particular someone in mind?"

Ada made a sound that could have been someone clicking their tongue in their mouth. I hadn't heard her make that sound before. Then again, I wouldn't have remembered even if she had, would I?

"Listen. You're not alone in there, Ray. Help is at hand, but you've got to follow along, okay? Can you do that for me, Ray?"

"What help?" I looked at the tape deck on the trolley. "The same help that hooked me up to the bypass?"

"They know what they're doing. Everything is going to plan, but you need to make sure you play ball, okay?"

"It would help if I knew what that plan was, Ada."

"No, it wouldn't, Ray. At least . . . not for the moment."

She made the clicking sound again. Or maybe it was the noise on the line. The interference was getting worse.

Then there was a sound like Ada had turned her head, the mouthpiece of her telephone brushing against her cheek as she looked at something.

"Ada?"

"Okay, sorry, I have to run. So, look, just hang in there. This is all part of the job, and I know you're good at it, so trust me when I say you'll find everything out in good time and this will all get straightened out."

There was a pause. I listened to the telephone. I could hear someone breathing and the breathing got faster.

"Sorry, Ray, I have to go," said Ada.

"Are you saying this is all part of a job?"

"Just like any other, Ray."

"Who is the target?"

Ada sighed. For a moment I wondered if I heard her chewing gum, but the line ticked and crackled and I couldn't be sure of anything.

"That's what I'm trying to find out, Ray."

I felt incorrect voltages go the wrong way around a circuit or two.

"That's not helpful. In fact, you could even call it a hindrance."

"Well, a gal can only do her best, right? You're a detective, detect! Keep your optics open and your audio receptors up and then you can report back and tell me what you've discovered."

"Including the identity of the person I need to get a little closer to than most?"

"Identity, location, favorite color, how they take their coffee. Whatever you need, chief, whatever you need."

I almost sighed but I caught my vocalizer just in time. I was making enough noise as it was. From beyond the closed door of the dressing room I could now hear the footsteps loud and clear. They were very close and the dressing room door wasn't particularly substantial, and with the whole place—whatever it was, wherever it was— as quiet as church on a Tuesday, whoever was coming was going to be able to hear me soon if they hadn't already.

I looked around. There was no other way out. This place didn't seem to have any windows.

The footsteps got closer.

"I've got to go, Ray," said Ada. She sounded flustered. Distracted. More than that, she sounded something else.

Real.

"Yeah, and I've got company coming," I said.

"Good luck," said Ada.

"I have a feeling I'm going to need it."

And then the telephone clicked dead and for a few seconds there was a silence as thick and heavy as a winter blanket on a cold night. And then the dial tone came back and the telephone buzzed in my ear. The tone was clear and loud with no interference.

I must have had the telephone in my hand when the dressing room door opened, because the first thing I did when I turned around to face it was pull the curly cable away from where it had got caught on my collar, and the second thing I did was put the receiver back on its cradle after the man with the gun in the doorway asked me to.

If this guy was Ada's promised help then I had to admit I was a little disappointed, what with the scowl on his face and the way his gun twitched like he really, truly wanted to shoot me with it. It was a strange gun too, like a piece of modern art, a sculpture of blown glass and wires that likely shot something that would be much more effective than bullets against my chassis.

"I'd put my hands up," I said, "but I'm a little attached to this drinks trolley."

The man's scowl twisted a little more. He was not quite middle-aged and the grimace couldn't disguise the pleasing angles of his face. He had hair to match and a sports coat that needed its own feature in *Life* magazine.

"You going to come with me, Sparks, or am I going to have to shoot you here and now?"

He jerked his gun sideways and I got the picture. I pushed my little trolley in front of me and he made a wide circle around the dressing room to give me the required space.

I paused at the doorway. He jerked his gun to the left.

"Move it, buster."

I did what he said.

17

The man with the gun walked behind me. At first I was glad of that fact, as it meant I didn't have to look at his jacket, but after a little while it became obvious this arrangement was not without problems. I didn't know where I was going and he had to keep giving me directions and I wasn't entirely sure he knew his way around the place any better than I did. More than twice he told me to push my trolley to the left only for this direction to be followed by a call to *hold on just one gosh-darned minute!* and there were a few other turnarounds accompanied by a selection of phrases including, *Oh, for Pete's sake, you think I'd know this place by now* and *she didn't sign me up for a job like this one* and one that caught my attention in particular, which was *dammit, Sparks, why does life have to be so difficult?*

I didn't say anything. He was having a bad enough day as it was and I didn't want to distract him further, not least of all because his grip on his magical pea shooter had been tight when we left the dressing room and I could only imagine how much tighter it was now.

Finally he told me to stop in the middle of another concrete block corridor and he said "please" when he did. I obliged and watched as he paced, the gun now pointed in every other direction than me as he got his bearings. I suppose I could have extricated myself right then and there but I liked the *please* bit. If I was going to be held up by a gangster then I liked one with a little class. There were too many lowlifes in Los Angeles without any manners. I didn't know how I knew that. It must have been on my permanent store, a bit of general information along with more formal stuff about how to be a detective and basic forensic investigative techniques volumes one through six and a list of the national birds of the countries of Europe.

Luxembourg had the goldcrest, by the way, which had the scientific equivalent of two first names: *Regulus regulus*.

For some reason that made me think of someone I might have known once but then the feeling was gone and the business end of the ray gun was once more angled toward me and we resumed our grand journey.

After a few minutes of walking we arrived at our destination, coming out into a narrow room with a very high ceiling. The room was filled with coils of cable, and ladders of various extendable dimensions were stacked against the wall opposite a pair of very narrow and very high doors. One of the doors was ajar and from beyond streamed bright light.

I looked at my companion and in the light I saw he really was quite a looker and he had hair that was high and swept back and might just have been blown out of glass like his fancy gun—a gun that now swung loosely by his side.

The man smiled at me and then the smile snapped off and the gun came up too fast, like he was embarrassed at being caught out. Of course, what he really needed to be embarrassed about was the jacket he was wearing. I took another look and then wondered if I could ask to have the lights turned off again.

"Inside," he said through a set of perfect teeth and through lips that moved as much as his pompadour, which is to say, not a lot.

I nodded and poked my trolley through the gap in the door and then I made the gap a little wider with my free hand as I stepped through.

"You'd make a good ventriloquist," I said.

"That's enough talking."

"My point exactly."

I wheeled the trolley a little farther and then I stopped where I was. My guide stepped into the room behind me and then he slid past and he turned and walked backward, keeping the gun level with me as he moved toward the guy who was standing in what seemed to be a library of a late Edwardian country house.

"Relax, Peterman," he said, a tall party in a black suit and with black hair. "No need to be on edge. Everything is under control."

The man with the gun—Peterman—stopped and made to glance over his shoulder at his friend, only to realize that this would mean he couldn't look at me at the same time, so he sort of leaned back and half-turned, his eyes swiveling in their sockets as he tried for the impossible.

I looked around the big room, which might have looked like an Edwardian country library but was anything but. Sure, there were chairs and the walls were lined with leather-bound spines, but from my position by the big doors I could see that's all they were. The books were fake, and the library was only half a room. It sat, disconnected from any kind of country manor, on a stage six inches from a floor of black painted cement covered with scuffs and marks and bits of old tape. There was scaffolding around the place and ladders and folding chairs and folding tables. The ceiling was somewhere high above, mostly hidden from view by a suspended metal framework from which sprung an array of lamps and lights like multicolored flowers. Ropes and chains hung down from the rig and were safely affixed to the walls.

It looked so much like a film set that I decided that's what it was, albeit one that hadn't seen an active production for some time. There was an atmosphere of disuse about the place and the air felt heavy and dusty with just a hint of damp. High above the only lights that were on gave out a comfortable yellowish-white and when I turned my audio receptors up I could hear them fizz a little.

"Well, listen, *bub*," said Peterman, "you know what happened last time. *And* the time before that. So you'll forgive me if I don't carry a little insurance around with me." He waggled the gun in front of himself. It looked heavy.

The man in the black suit winced, then lifted his chin and directed his attention at me.

"I'm sorry, Ray," he said. "You'll have to forgive Mr. Peterman. He's been under a lot of pressure recently, shall we say." He paused and tilted his head. "How are you feeling?"

It was a strange question to put to a mechanical man, but there was something about the man in the black suit that was familiar and he had an air about him that suggested he knew exactly who—and what—he was talking to.

I opened my mouth grille and then I thought of the number seventeen for some reason and I closed the grille again. It made a clicking sound. The two looked at me and then each other.

"How is he doing?" asked the man in the black suit of his friend with the gun.

"Maybe a short circuit or two," said Peterman. With the gun aimed at my chest he came close enough to touch and whatever nervousness there had been before was now absent. He looked me up and down, and then he looked down at the tape recorder on the trolley. He gave the dials a tap with a fingernail. "But he's otherwise in good shape," he said. "His memory reset is complete and the new tape is running."

I watched the two of them. I felt my circuits get hot. I wanted to loosen my collar. I wanted to take off my hat and wipe down my forehead with a handkerchief. All of this was unnecessary as I didn't sweat and I could withstand a temperature hot enough to melt a school bus without too much difficulty, but that didn't stop me from lifting my hat up and checking the head band and then putting it back where I had found it. Peterman watched me from by the trolley.

"I can understand you may have some questions, Ray," said the man in the black suit. He hadn't moved from the stage but now he gestured to one of the easy chairs in the fake library. I didn't need to sit down but I thought matters might be expedited a little if I took his invitation so I moved to the stage and I stepped up onto it and I trailed out the cables from the trolley and I sat down. The man in the black suit smiled and nodded and he moved one of the other easy chairs around so it was facing mine directly. He stood behind it with his hands on the top and his elbows locked.

"Now," he said, "we can begin."

"You got that right," I said. "And you can begin with telling me who you guys are and what this place is."

The man in the black suit laughed. "Ah, Raymond Electromatic, wonder that you are, a modern miracle with one small but essential problem. You can't remember a thing, thanks to that little tape in your chest. Thornton's final insoluble dilemma."

I pursed my lips. Or at least I felt like I did.

"But that does not present us with a problem, Ray," he continued, "because what I want is right here." He stood tall and walked to the edge of the stage. He pointed to the tape recorder. "Thanks to Mr. Peterman's expertise, we were able to save you before you had a catastrophic systems failure. We salvaged your tape as well, although in the process some of the data recorded during your last day was scrambled. But, as I said, this does not present us with any particular problem. All you have to do is unscramble it for me."

The man in the black suit waved a finger at Peterman. Peterman nodded and moved to the tape deck on the trolley.

I looked up at the man in the black suit. "Listen, pal, I don't know who you are or what you think you're doing, but I've had about as much as I can take. So you're going to tell me who you are and what's going on and maybe we can even have that conversation in a polite and civilized manner. But you seem to know me and if that's true then you know what I can do, so how about we work together to avoid any unpleasantness, okay?"

I went to stand up and there was a crack like a tree being struck by lightning and I found I couldn't move a single servo. My optics went green around the edges and white horizontal lines flickered across everything I saw. I got my optics over to where Peterman was standing by the trolley. He had both hands on the controls and was slowly twisting knobs in the clockwise direction and the dials above the tape reels were clicking as the needles within bounced against their upper limits.

I tried to speak but my vocalizer wasn't playing ball. I tried to make some adjustments to my systems but I got nothing except error codes five ways to Sunday.

The man in the black suit stepped around his easy chair and sat in it. Then he scooted himself forward so he was balanced on the very edge. He adjusted its position on the floor and drew himself closer to me.

Then he raised his right hand. He made it into a fist and then he uncurled his index finger and pointed it at my chest.

"My name is Special Agent Touch Daley," he said. "I work for the Department of Robot Labor."

Then his index finger broke at the middle joint and swung down on a hinge and I found myself looking down a metal barrel. A second later a silver probe telescoped out of the barrel and extended six inches before stopping.

"And," said Touch Daley, "we are going to start this conversation with a very simple question."

I wondered how I was going to answer his very simple question when I couldn't speak but then the silver probe extended again and entered one of the exposed data ports on my chest unit and the world exploded into amber shapes and my internal diagnostics told me what I already knew.

My system was compromised. My positronic brain was under somebody else's control. My permanent store was unlocked.

Touch Daley's voice boomed inside my head as his foggy silhouette loomed in front of my optics, nothing but a shadow cast against a world of white noise.

"Where," asked the shadow, "is Ada?"

18

And then I woke up and it was another beautiful day in Hollywood, California. Just like it always was, each and every morning when I woke in my alcove and the world was born anew.

But not this morning. Something was different.

Very different.

I wasn't standing in my alcove. I was standing in a small room made of concrete blocks painted a dull forest green. The floor was cement and slightly damp. There were no windows but the room was lit by a single unshaded bulb hanging from a cable hanging from the ceiling. Beside me was a silver wheeled trolley on which a portable tape machine purred. As I watched the reels slowly turn I saw the needles in the dials above those reels jump almost in time to my thoughts.

These things were perhaps the least of my problems. My

primary concern was the man leaning in the doorway. He was wearing a jacket in desperate need of being burned and buried and he was holding a gun that didn't shoot bullets and that gun was pointing right at me.

"Good morning, Sparks," he said. A smile appeared and then was gone. Whoever he was he looked tired and I told him the same. That reignited the smile and it was joined by something that might be called a guffaw, if only there had been an atom of humor in it.

"If I look tired I can only imagine how you must feel," he said.

I thought that was a strange thing to say and I told him that as well but that just made him shake his head and I thought I should maybe have asked Peterman for coffee and the morning paper instead.

Peterman.

I said his name and he looked up and the smile came back and now it had a certain warmth to it. He nodded and I saw his grip on his funny-looking gun relax.

"Hey, Sparks, things are looking up! You're starting to remember. Listen—"

Peterman paused. He pulled at his bottom lip with his free hand and then when he was done with his face he used the same hand to pull at the lapel of his jacket. I wondered whether I should give him a hand to pull it off completely and then maybe we could see what his ray gun would do to it.

Not a lot, I thought. It was the kind of gun designed to shoot robots with.

"Listen," said Peterman, starting himself up again, "I'm sorry what he's doing to you, but you're holding up, and that's good. There's not long to go now and I think we'll have all we need, okay?"

I said nothing. Peterman nodded and he rolled his neck.

"Okay," he said. Then he twitched the gun. "Better not keep him waiting."

He twitched the gun a second time and I walked out of the room and into a maze of corridors.

I led the way. I didn't know where I was going but, somehow, I remembered.

I led Peterman into a large room with a low stage on which was constructed a passable replica of a library from an Edwardian country house. Standing on the library's red and purple paisley carpet next to a pair of large easy chairs was a tall man in a black suit with black hair.

"Welcome back, Ray," he said. He walked behind one of the easy chairs and patted the top of it with both hands. "How about we get ourselves comfortable and have a chat?"

I looked at Peterman. He was looking dead ahead but he caught my glance and he lifted his chin up and his eyes went back to the front but I think I got the message.

I didn't know anything about him other than his surname and terrible taste in casual jackets, but I was starting to like him.

For a moment I remembered a conversation out in the hills behind Hollywood, standing in the heat, standing under an oak. I remembered the sound of the birds and the smell of the dirt and the smell of his aftershave.

And for a moment I remembered lying on a hard metal surface, lying in a box on wheels that moved, and

I remembered the sound of the engine and the screech of the tires and the smell of dust and gasoline.

"Ray?"

I adjusted my optics and the fakery in front of me swam back into focus. I looked down at the tape machine on the trolley. It was connected to my chest unit by a thin double cable. My chest panel was open and my shirt was unbuttoned. The reels on the tape machine turned but the reels inside my chest were still.

I looked up at the man in the black suit.

"I don't know who you are," I said, "but I'm guessing I have you to thank for this. If I came to the end of my memory tape . . . well, let's just say I'm not sure I would want to know what that was like."

The needles on the dials on the tape machine twitched in time with my words.

"Yes, it was close for a moment there, Ray," said the man in the black suit. "We managed to save your systems from a truly catastrophic failure. You should count yourself lucky."

There was something about his tone I didn't like.

I kept my mouth grille shut.

He gestured to the easy chair. "Please?"

I cleared my throat. It sounded like a forklift truck dragging a dumpster and it echoed in the big room. The man in the black suit was watching me carefully but I was doing the same to him.

"Believe me, I'm grateful for the help," I said. I moved toward the stage. I left the trolley where it was and I let the cables trail behind me. "But I'm going to need to know why I needed the help in the first place. And maybe once we get that cleared up we can work on the little problem of who you are and who you work for and how you know me and where I am and what you intend to do to fix the situation, whatever the situation is, because at the moment I don't rightly know."

Down on the main floor, Peterman had his head held high and the gun held tight. I had a feeling he was putting that on but I wasn't sure if it was for me or his charming friend.

"All will become clear, Ray," said the man in the black suit. "In fact, that's exactly what I'm here to do. I'm here to help you remember. You see, your memory tape was damaged when we rescued you. There's important information about our case on it. The data has been scrambled, but it's all still there. We just need your help to extract it."

I looked at Peterman and he nodded so I sat in the easy chair. He seemed to know what was going on even if I didn't.

I sat with my hands on my knees and the cables trailing to the portable tape deck. Peterman moved to the trolley and stashed his gun on the side. Then he wheeled the whole thing around so his back was to me and the device was hidden from the stage.

"Now then, Mr. Electromatic," said his friend in the black suit. He walked around the other easy chair and lowered himself in it and crossed one knee over the other. Then he seemed to get a better idea and he uncrossed his legs and scooted forward so he was balanced on the edge of the chair and then he dragged the whole thing forward until he was directly facing me, close enough to touch.

"We'll make this quick and easy and maybe we'll find that answer rattling around in your circuits somewhere," he said.

I might have come up with a question or two about

that particular statement, but my logic gates got a little distracted by a sudden influx of data, a stream of numbers and code that were wrapped around themselves inside of a signal that overwhelmed my systems to such a degree that nearly every nonessential function packed its bags and turned off the lights and set sail for an early weekend.

That included my motors and their servos, and that certainly included my vocalizer. I couldn't even work the little flap behind my mouth grille.

And as the man in the black suit leaned forward my optical register overloaded and started scaling the world around me down to nothing but constituent colors and shapes and then even the colors faded away until I was left with shadows and static.

One of the shadows was the man in the black suit. I knew that much even though it took nearly all of my available megacycles to make him out. He seemed closer and it felt like he was touching my chest panel and then it felt like his hand was passing right through me.

"I'll ask you again, Ray," said the shadow.

I was about ready to say goodnight when my audio receptors captured his question and then all kinds of things lit up inside me.

"Where," he asked, "is Ada?"

19

And then I woke up and it was another beautiful day in Hollywood, California. Just like it always was, each and every morning when I woke in my alcove and the world was born anew.

But not this morning. Something was different.

Very different.

I remembered.

I remembered everything.

Fresco Peterman was at the door of the storage room and he had the gun but he knew something was different too because when I awakened from my digitized slumber he pushed himself off the doorway and the gun hung loosely from his hand.

"Ray? Hey, Sparks, you in there? Wake up, big fella."

I turned the lights in my optics up a notch and that made Peterman take a step back before he breathed a sigh of relief.

"And good morning to you too," he said.

I didn't speak. I was busy cogitating. Correlating. I did some hard math to clear my circuits and then ran the data again but I'd been right the first time.

I grabbed the trolley with my portable tape recorder on it with one hand and gave it a little push. Peterman's eyes fell to the tape recorder and then they were back on me.

"I've got it," I said.

Peterman nodded. "And?"

"I know who the target is."

Peterman grinned. He clicked the fingers of the hand that wasn't holding the gun and then he tapped me on the shoulder, but he did it carefully like he thought he might get an electric shock. He took a step back toward the door.

"Then let's bust this joint," he said.

He disappeared into the corridor.

I followed.

I knew what was happening.

I remembered.

None of this made me happy in the slightest.

Special Agent Touch Daley was waiting for us on the library set. He stood on the stage with his hands neatly folded in front of his belt buckle and a smile on his face and a downward tilt to his face that told me an awful lot about his state of mind.

He was confident. Not happy, because in a job like his you didn't have the luxury of being happy. But you could take a certain satisfaction from performing your assigned task with a level of success. That was why he was here, after all. He was the best man for the job.

Scratch that, he was the *only* man for the job and he wasn't a man at all. He was a machine, like me but not like me at all. He was number seventeen. The significance of that I didn't yet understand and it was part of something bigger that I sure didn't remember. I suspected Fresco Peterman knew and I suspected he would tell me in good time. For the moment, I just had to follow the notion that while I didn't know exactly what had gone on before I had a fair idea of what was going to happen next.

"Mr. Electromatic," said Touch Daley. "It's good to see you again. I'm very pleased you could be here for this little conversation."

His politeness was interesting, in an academic kind of way. Maybe it was how he kept control. Cool, calm, collected—you know, the usual. He was a man—a *robot*—in charge of the situation and he knew it and he could steer the whole shebang any way he pleased.

Except I was about to disabuse him of that idea, and fast.

"Always a pleasure, Agent Daley," I said. I moved to the stage while Fresco Peterman kept his gun level at my chassis and kept his step close to mine. When I got up next to Daley I pulled my little trolley up against the riser the fake library sat on and Peterman turned his attention to it like he always did.

If Touch Daley paused at all, it was then, and it was just for a moment, and while there was nothing happening that he didn't want to happen, I wondered if perhaps he had a kind of electronic intuition like I had. It may have been part of my programming. Something inherited from Professor Thornton's template, or something cooked up by him to make me better at being a detective. I didn't know.

But if Professor Thornton had passed that power on to me, he sure as hell hadn't passed it on to Special Agent Touch Daley, because Special Agent Touch Daley may have been a robot but he wasn't one that Professor Thornton had a hand in.

Seems like I'd remembered quite a lot.

Daley made a gesture to the easy chair on the left side of the library and when I was settled in he smiled and nodded and unfolded his hands and he moved the other easy chair so it was in front of mine and he sat in it and he scooted forward so our knees were almost touching.

"Now, Mr. Electromatic, we've got a lot to discuss," Daley said, "and I'm sure you have a lot of questions you want answered yourself."

"Oh, I think I have few answers already," I said. "But you're right. There are some matters I still need to have cleared up."

Daley paused. He looked at me and he clicked his tongue. It was a neat trick, starting with the fact that he had a tongue to click in the first place. He was a mechanical man and he was a work of art.

I wondered what the catch was.

Then he glanced at Peterman. Peterman nodded at him and he glanced at me and then he turned to the tape recorder and waved his hands over the control like he was about to conjure a rabbit, if only he had a top hat at hand.

"Okay, Ray," said Daley. "Let's start with an easy one."

"Where's Ada?" I asked.

Daley sat more upright, if that were possible. His mouth opened but I got in first.

"It's a question I've been asking myself," I said. "It's interesting that you don't know, given that it was your department who boxed her up and shipped her out."

Daley licked his bottom lip. "Mr. Peterman, I think our guest is ready for the next phase."

He stopped. He looked. I looked.

Peterman had the ray gun in his hand again and it was pointed at a robot sitting in an easy chair and that robot wasn't me.

I knew I liked him.

Daley adjusted himself in the easy chair and he even lifted his hands and showed me his palms. I took a look. The workmanship was nothing short of miraculous.

"Ray, Ray," he said. "It looks like you're coming back to us. That's good. That's *excellent*."

"I'm sure it is," I said. "But not for you."

"Listen, Ray, I don't know—"

"No, that's just it. You don't know. Specifically, where Ada is. And like I said that's an interesting fact because the Department of Robot Labor should have her. Except you don't work for the Department of Robot Labor. No, you work for another organization entirely."

Peterman chuckled. It was so loud I thought he was practicing lines for one of his movies.

"International Automatic," I said. "Mean anything to you, bub?"

Daley's smile came back. It was a narrow and reptilian thing and for one moment I was glad I wasn't a robot like Daley and I hadn't been built to make an expression like that.

"I'll take that as a yes," I said.

"You're a clever machine," said Daley. "International

Automatic has a great need for clever machines like you."

"Yeah, I thought that was coming. Try to tell me that you're on my side and you have been all along."

Daley let his hands drop and he used one of them to point to the tape recorder. "I saved you, Ray. If I hadn't found you in the alleyway in time your memory would have suffered irreparable damage. Even your permanent store could have been compromised."

"Oh, it was," I said. "By you. You went poking around in my memory to see if I knew where my boss was. Only you haven't found anything out because I don't know. But you can't accept that—because if I didn't get Ada out of the office, then who did? Oh, the office was raided by the Department of Robot Labor, a department you've been posing as the head of, presumably replacing the real Special Agent Touch Daley. You organized the raid yourself and you led it yourself. Only someone screwed up your plans. Your boys were taking orders from someone else that night and after you were done loading Ada up into the vans she was driven off into the night and *away* from your clutches."

Touch Daley didn't say much. He just moved his lips around, which I took as a sign that he was listening at least.

"Of course you didn't know that, not then. You watched the vans get loaded and then you got an anonymous tip that you should go take a look in the alleyway. That's where you found me. At first you thought I was snooping and that's just a piece of luck. But later—when you found out your delivery vans didn't make it to the intended destination— you figured I was there to supervise my little bit of subterfuge. My memory tape was running out but that's okay because you had one of your double agents, Fresco

Peterman, on hand with his technical know-how-can-do.

"Which brings us to an Edwardian country library. Maybe you've malfunctioned, set yourself in a logical loop because your system is stuck on an idea and ideas can be hard to shift. Trust me, I know how it feels. I must know where Ada is because I got her out, except I don't know where she is because I didn't get her out." I glanced at Peterman. "I hope he's paying you market rates because you'll be here until 1986 at the very earliest before Touch Daley Seventeen breaks out of his program cycle."

"Very good," said Daley.

"Well, I am a detective," I said. "I'm just doing my job."

Daley laughed. "Ray, you haven't done that job in a long while."

"There you may have a point. In fact, I'm on a case right now. And thanks to you, I've identified the target."

Daley slid forward again on the easy chair. Peterman kept him covered.

"Oh?" said Daley. "And are you going to tell me?" He rubbed his jaw with a hand. "No, wait, I've got that wrong. Say, Peterman, what happens in your movies? Isn't it the bad guy who has the good guy in his grasp and he reveals his diabolical masterplan before the plucky hero makes his daring and unsuspected escape?"

"You're right," I said, "except for one important point. See, I don't have a masterplan, diabolical or otherwise. All I have is the job, and that requires two pieces of information. One, the identity of the target. Two, their location. In this case, I now have one, but not the other, and the way you've been asking me the same question over and over for who knows how long suggests you don't have the information I need."

Daley steepled his fingers under his chin and he used those fingers to push his head up enough for him to look down his long nose at me.

"Fascinating, Ray. Truly fascinating." He spread his open hands. "I think we've reached an impasse, unless you want to ask me the question, just to be sure. Perhaps we can come to some . . . arrangement."

"And there's the next part. An offer of assistance. Join forces and together we can defeat the enemy."

"Perhaps we can, Ray. Perhaps we can."

"Not when the enemy is IA."

Daley laughed again. It sounded more realistic than my version.

"I'd love to know why you think IA is the enemy, Ray," said Daley. "What IA plans will benefit the entire world."

"No," I said, "what IA plans will benefit IA. See, it seems I've met your company before, and I learned a thing or two. Of course I can't remember any of that but thanks to our little meetings here I think I've brought myself up to speed. IA wants to restart the robot revolution, only that's exactly what it will be. Replace people with robots and you solve a lot of problems. Replace *everybody* with robots and you have a mechanical planet free of crime and disease and sadness and also free of life and love and art and emotion." I sat back in my chair. "So yes, IA is the enemy."

"You may be a master assassin, Ray, but even you can't kill an entire organization."

"I don't have to. I just need to cut off the head. Kill the boss."

The third laugh. "You think I'm going to tell you who the boss is?"

"I told you, I already know their identity."

Daley cocked his head. He regarded me with eyes that glistened with moisture and yet were artificial, just like mine.

I moved forward on my own easy chair. My knees touched Daley's.

"Where is Ada?" I asked.

Daley smiled his snake smile. "That was exactly what I was wanting *you* to tell *me*."

I sat back. I shrugged. "Program loop, told you," I said. Then I stood up. Then I made to leave and then Daley stood up and he reached forward and his smile was as black as coal and as cold as the ocean and from his extended index finger came the silver probe.

He snarled as he lunged at me and then he screamed as he was enveloped by blue sparking fire. He fell back into the easy chair with a thump, because a dead robot is a dead weight.

Peterman stepped up onto the stage, the discharged ray gun glowing in his hand.

"More will be coming," he said. "And fast too. You kept him talking a good while but that will have alerted IA."

"Got anything?"

"Maybe," he said, nodding at the tape recorder on the trolley. "We'll check it out. But first, we'd better at least move him. If they come looking and don't find number seventeen that might slow them down a little."

I bent down and picked up Touch Daley Seventeen. He was as heavy as a broken heart. Then I stepped down to the studio floor and headed for the door. Peterman wound my cables up in one hand and pushed the trolley behind me.

"Out and left," he said.

I followed his directions.

20

I went left and I kept going with Touch Daley Seventeen in my arms and Peterman at my shoulder. As we walked I thought about the situation. I thought about what I had found out. I thought about the target.

The head of International Automatic.

Ada.

I decided to halt a few processes in my positronic core for a moment or two. My circuits felt like they were about to blow smoke at any moment and I needed to focus on the job at hand, which was getting out of wherever we were and getting away from the forces of IA, which were, apparently, on the way.

"Here," said Peterman.

I stopped. We were at a door. It was locked, and while Peterman got to work on it with a set of keys that emerged from his jacket, I looked around. There was nothing particularly memorable about where we were. It was a corridor like the others, wide and concrete, the only variation being the color. The locked door was painted green and it had a silver door handle and when Peterman opened it I saw that it led to a room that was narrow and rectangular, windowless. It was a glorified closet, the kind a janitor would keep his brooms and mops and buckets in and perhaps a thermos of coffee and a pail of lunch and a stack of well-read magazines under the chair.

None of these things was in the closet, but it was far from empty. In fact, it was quite full.

I bent down and let Touch Daley Seventeen join his fallen comrades.

The carcasses of the sixteen previous incarnations of Special Agent Touch Daley were arranged neatly along the walls, all sitting up, some stacked three deep. The deactivated robot bodies slumped in each other's arms like passed-out drunks. Each was the same as the other in their black suits and black ties and white shirts and they all stared with open dead eyes and they all still wore their tight black trilby hats.

All but one. He was by the door, getting close and personal with another one of himself, and his head was bare.

I must have taken in the view from the doorway for quite a while, because eventually Peterman coughed and then he cleared his throat.

"My words exactly," I said. "You've been busy."

"*We've* been busy, Sparks," said Peterman. "Speaking of, we need to split and see what we've got on the tape."

I wasn't sure what he meant but I didn't want to confuse matters right now. Peterman would tell me later and I had to prioritize.

"Splitting sounds easier said than done." I pointed at the tape deck on the trolley. The reels were still turning and the dials were still flickering. "This thing is going to slow me down. And what happens when it runs out? We'll be back to square one—or I will be, at least."

Peterman's face broke into a grin. "Hey, Sparks, you don't think this very rich and very handsome star of the silver screen hasn't thought of that?"

He reached into the inside pocket of his jacket and felt around. I watched him but the movement of the patterned fabric did strange things to my optics so I returned my attention to the seventeen deactivated Touch Daleys laid out before me.

Was IA on the way? Did they somehow know that the latest number had become the latest victim of Fresco Peterman's trigger finger?

And what was the catch? These robots were perfect replicas of human beings. They were utterly unlike anything Thornton had dreamed of. If they were the work of IA, the company was decades ahead in technology.

So . . . what was the catch?

"Okay, show time," said Peterman. I turned to face him and found him brandishing not the ray gun but a screwdriver.

I raised an eyebrow, or at least I tried my darnedest.

"We going to twist our way out of this?" I asked.

Peterman's grin got an inch wider on either side. "Got it in one, Sparks. Got it in one."

A half hour later we emerged into the sunshine. Peterman

stood and blinked and shielded his eyes against the sudden glare. I adjusted my optics and waited for the retino-active photo cell receivers to cool down a bit. Two seconds later I was good to go.

Go where, I wasn't sure. But I was up and running and freed from the portable tape recorder and the umbilical cord. My memory tape wound on in my chest unit and it was as fresh as a cool evening breeze and I had Fresco Peterman to thank for that.

Peterman, and his collection of robot parts. He'd known just what he was doing as he got to work with his screwdriver, at first searching the seventeen Touch Daleys until he found one with a particular component intact. While they all looked fine from the outside, most of them were cooked on the inside, thanks to the ray gun.

I planned on asking him about that gun and about how he knew what he was looking for. Yes, the two of us were going to have quite a chat and with a bit of luck I might even remember it this time.

The result of Peterman's efforts was the installation of a neutron flow polarity reverser in my chest unit. I had room thanks to my curved replacement chest panel. The reverser did just that—it allowed Peterman to rewind my memory tape and set it going, and with the data from the portable deck still intact, I remembered what had happened ever since I'd gone looking for him in Bay City.

I had gaps—some big ones—but it allowed me to get the hell out of that place with Peterman hot on the tails of my trench coat and now, as I stood in the sunshine, I looked out across a flat expanse of cracking concrete surrounded by tall beige buildings big enough to build steamships in and—

And a vague recollection of a wet night and a small talkative man sitting next to me in my car, pointing to the back of someone else as that someone else trotted up some stairs and disappeared into a building and—

And then that fragment disappeared as well.

Peterman nodded to himself. "So we're at—"

"Playback Pictures," I said. "The studio lot."

"Ah, okay, so you know about Playback Pictures."

"Call it déjà vu."

"Okay, great, a robot with déjà vu," said Peterman. "That's no problem, no problem at all."

"I suggest we quit this conversation while we're ahead and work on exiting Playback Pictures a little faster."

That was when I heard it. Peterman heard it too. We both turned around toward the sound.

It was a car, moving fast, somewhere out of sight, among the deserted buildings.

"Two's company, three's a crowd," said Peterman. "Come on."

We skirted the building and aimed for north.

We found the car a little farther on and we watched it from the shadows near another studio block. It was long and black and it had stopped in the middle of road that wound around the backlot.

Special Agent Touch Daley stood by the open driver's door. Model Eighteen wasn't doing much of anything but looking around. I wondered why this was and Peterman frowned like he was wondering the same. And then we got our answer.

Another car arrived. Same make and model, same color. Same driver.

But this one brought passengers. One in the front, two in the back. As it pulled up alongside the first car, another automobile came in along the same access road. And another. And another.

Touch Daley Eighteen was joined by Nineteen through Thirty and I didn't like those odds at all.

I backed up a little and I pulled Peterman with me.

"I thought they only came out one at a time," I said.

Peterman didn't look happy. "You and me both, Sparks. This is bad news. They must be really desperate to get that information out of you."

"Information I don't have," I said.

Information I wasn't sure I wanted to find, I said to nobody but myself.

Touch Daley and his electronic brothers had now gathered around the first car and it looked like they were making plans. If we were going to make our escape we had to make it pretty quick.

"Listen," said Peterman. "They think I'm still working for them. I can go out there and buy you some time. I can get the tape out and get it analyzed, and we can rendezvous later."

"You want to go out there and face a baker's dozen of those things?"

Peterman's hand disappeared into his jacket pocket and came out with a small leather wallet. He flipped it open with the fingers of one hand and held it out to me with practiced ease. I looked at a passport-sized photo of him and a small card of information with a signature—Touch Daley's—at the bottom.

"I'm still a DORL agent—which means I'm still an IA agent."

"Events seem to have progressed," I said. "You think that will work?"

Peterman slapped me on the shoulder. "One way to find out," he said, and before I could stop him he dashed out of the alley and headed toward the gang of one. I watched him for a couple of moments as he was surrounded by the identical men in black and then I turned around and I looked for another way out.

I checked my fresh memory tape. I had twenty-three hours and change.

Suddenly a day didn't seem like a very long time at all.

21

I had twenty-three hours and ten minutes left by the time I found my exit strategy and all the way back to Hollywood I lamented the time wasted.

Playback Pictures was in Studio City and that was too much of a walk back to Hollywood, especially with my personal countdown clock ticking away in my chest.

I had found a small fleet of vans and trucks parked in a lot behind another of the outbuildings. The vehicles were all big and slow but any would have done in a pinch had their tires not been flat. Even if I had been able to start any of them, the sound of a disused diesel motor firing into reluctant life would have brought six brace of Touch Daleys tearing around the corner before I'd gotten into second gear.

With time being of an essence I decided to trust that Fresco Peterman knew as much about being a double agent as he did about setting up the neutron flow polarity reverser inside my chest. I doubled back around to where the new arrivals had parked their cars.

I was in luck. The four cars were parked in a row and their occupants were nowhere to be seen. I didn't waste a single kilocycle as I hoofed across the lot and opened the driver's door of the car nearest and got inside and got it hotwired and got it pointing in the right direction and got the accelerator pushed all the way to the floor.

I drove it to Hollywood and I kept an optic out for trouble along the way, but nothing happened en route to the Cahuenga Building except someone ahead of me changed lanes without indicating and someone else showed his annoyance by leaning on the horn for a good deal longer than he needed to. But followed from Playback Pictures, I was not. Peterman had thrown the others off the scent, at least for now.

Why I headed for the office I wasn't sure but I knew Peterman was going to get in touch and I hoped soon. He had the tapes. He had the answers.

I had to admit there was a good deal of hoping going on there.

I rolled down Hollywood Boulevard and kept on going past the office. Los Angeles was already baking under the late morning sun and as I looked around me I could see nothing in particular going except life on Earth. There were cars and there were people and both of these things were either moving or were parked. The office building sat back on the corner like it had sat for the best part of the last century and that was all there was to it.

I went on for another block down the street and then I

pulled the car parallel to the curb and brought the thing to a halt. I turned it off. I sat in the driver's seat. I kept my optics on the rearview mirror and I asked myself what I expected to see. I didn't have much of an answer.

Then I glanced down at my right hand and I found the fingers reaching for the telephone that wasn't there, which was the strangest thing because I could hear a telephone ringing.

I turned around in my seat and looked out the back like maybe the rearview mirror hadn't been showing me a true picture. Then I looked out of both sides of the car and then I looked through the front windshield and then I knew where the telephone was, which was in the car parked in front of me.

My car.

I got out of Daley's government-issue boat and closed the door and I looked at the car in front of it and I read the license plate. It was mine, all right. There was desert dust around the tires and even some leaves, and when I walked around to the front I saw there was a ticket under the windshield wiper. The telephone was still ringing so I left the ticket where it was and I opened the driver's door and I got in and I closed the door and I picked up the telephone.

And I paused, because while I wanted to speak to the party I knew was on the other end, I didn't want to have to confirm what I had learned.

That the boss of International Automatic was my target.

That the boss of International Automatic was Ada.

The telephone clicked in my ear. I didn't speak.

Then someone cleared their throat and a male voice asked: "Ah . . . hullo?"

I paused some more.

"Sparks?"

"Peterman?"

"Sparks, buddy, for a moment there I thought I'd got the wrong number."

"Where are you?"

"What? Where do you think? Come on, use that electronic loaf of yours."

I turned around in the driver's seat. There was nobody around. Farther back, down at the lights, stood the Cahuenga Building and inside it was my office.

I turned back around. "They left the phone plugged in, then."

"They sure did."

"Which means they have it tapped."

"That also occurred to me, Sparks. I'm no amateur—I swept the place. It's clean."

"It may be at that end," I said, "but who knows where else they might be listening."

I heard Peterman sigh. "Listen, come up. We can talk, mano a . . . well, roboto, or something. I have the tape analyzed and all the answers you need."

"Analyzed already? How?"

Peterman snickered into the phone. "Let's just say I have a very capable acquaintance."

"I'll be right up," I said, and then I hung up.

And then I sat in the car and the traffic moved on the street. I looked in the mirrors—all of them. There were no men in black suits coming for me and the office building back on the corner was quiet.

I wasn't sure who Peterman meant when he said he had

a very capable acquaintance, but I added that question to the long list that was already heating up my rhetorical analysis capacitors.

I got out. I closed the door. Then I saw the parking ticket on the windshield again. I peeled it out from under the wiper and took a look. A six-dollar fine. Then I checked the date, and then I opened the car door a crack and slid the ticket inside and then I turned and headed to the office to meet Peterman.

I'd been kept inside Playback Pictures a whole month.

Now it was time for Peterman to tell me why.

22

I went up to the office the only way I knew how, which was via the elevator and then along the corridor and then through the door. My circuits did a pretty good simulation of a nervous sweat as I headed up but the lobby was empty along with the elevator and the hallway. This wasn't unusual. That the building was quiet and the tenants kept to themselves was one of the reasons Thornton had selected it as the home of the Electromatic Detective Agency. But with the hoo-ha a month ago and the place filled with federal agents and their unsmiling demeanors I wondered whether there was anyone left in the building to meet or whether the landlord had been saddled with a whole lot of lease-termination notices.

The main door was unlocked as it usually was. From the hallway I could see nothing in particular through the frosted glass, but I was glad it was intact. I imagined the men from DORL would have been rough when it came to dismantling the place.

I stepped through. Everything was where it should have been. The rug. The hatstand. The desk with the comfortable chair behind it and the less comfortable ones in front. There were two low bookcases lined with books and there was a filing cabinet filled with files. Both looked unmolested.

Fresco Peterman was leaning on the side of the desk closest to the telephone and when I walked in he pushed himself off.

"Ray, good to see you."

I closed the door. I walked toward him across the rug. A quarter of the way there I glanced at the door that connected the outer office to the computer room, and when I hit the halfway mark I looked over to the wall opposite, where the hidden door led to the tape archive.

Peterman watched me. "Yeah, they did a number," he said. "Take a look."

He led the way to the hidden door and opened it and then he stood back with his arms folded. I walked past him and walked inside and then I stopped because there wasn't much reason to go any farther.

The room was empty. Oh, sure, there were shelves in there. Lots of them. And there was even a light with a bulb and a shade. But that was it. I didn't remember how many tapes were stored here and what time period they represented—according to my sensory inputs this was the first time I had ever laid optics on the place—but the room looked like it could fit a lot.

Touch Daley had them all. I wondered whether that meant he had handed them to the Department of Robot

Labor or International Automatic, but then I stopped wondering because the question was irrelevant.

The two organizations were one in the same.

Which made the present whereabouts of Ada an interesting conundrum. She was the boss of IA. Someone had made damn sure they didn't have her. I turned around in the room and I looked at Peterman standing in the doorway with his lips puckered like he was waiting for a kiss and I thought about his very capable acquaintance. I didn't know who that was but I was starting to get an idea. Because Peterman's only other employer, at least as far as I knew, aside from DORL/IA, was Ada herself.

I left a reticulated logarithmic pattern analysis manifest cooking on that one as I walked out of the storeroom and headed to the computer room. On the way across I turned up my audio receptors but all I could hear was the tick of the clock that was above the door on the other side. I stopped there and counted the ticks and then opened the door and stepped through.

The computer room was empty. Somehow it looked smaller, now that Ada was gone. All that was left of her were a series of outlines, formed by faded paintwork, that crawled across the walls. She was there, but in silhouette only. My alcove was gone. They'd even taken the little round table and the chair.

I walked around the room. I counted the power outlets, of which there were a great deal, and the other sockets as well—telephone, telex, and a few I would have needed to look up. They'd disconnected everything and taken her away in pieces and had left not a single stray wire in the place.

I completed my third orbit and then I stopped. Peterman

was standing in the doorway with his arms folded and a look on his face that was ever so slightly satisfied.

I knew why, too.

"They don't have her," I said.

Peterman unfolded his arms and he clicked his fingers with both hands. "They most certainly do not."

I turned to the window and looked out. The brick building was there. In the gap below, the alleyway from which I'd watched as my boss was transported away.

I turned back to Peterman. "You do."

"Not me. *We*. I mean, not you and *me*, we, but me and her, *we*. Listen, don't worry, Ada is as safe as houses. Just don't ask me where she is, exactly, because I'm as in the dark on that one as you and our friend Touch Daley and his numerous successors."

I nodded. "So as soon as Ada found out they were coming to get her—or rather, that Touch Daley was coming to get her—she made plans for her own escape. And you arranged it?"

"I did," said Peterman.

I pointed in the general direction of the storage room. "What about my memory tapes?"

Peterman bobbed his head side to side like he was trying to pick out a stuffed toy prize from a fairground attraction. "Well, no, the tapes, we don't have. I got Ada out but that was a stretch as it was. The tapes went into another van and that van reached the original destination." Then he clicked his fingers on both hands and he pointed two index fingers at me along with a smile that I was sure had a tendency to make the front row of a cinema swoon into their popcorn. "But don't worry," he said. "They have your tapes but they can't do anything with them. Ada was no slouch. Those tapes are encrypted, my friend."

"Encrypted?"

"Totally scrambled without the right decoding key," said Peterman. He tapped the side of his head. "And that key is locked up inside your cranium, Ray. You're the only one able to decode them. Not even Ada can crack it."

"Another safeguard," I said.

"Hey," said Peterman, "Ada is one smart cookie."

I nodded, then I returned my available processing time to the issue of Touch Daley.

Touch Daleys, *plural*.

"Touch Daley is head of the Department of Robot Labor," I said. "Or he was. The real Touch Daley. Until IA took him out and swapped in their own version."

Peterman nodded. "To get their robot revolution on track, IA needed to infiltrate the DORL and gain access to their files on the original robot program."

"And DORL was never disbanded, just, what, forgotten?"

Peterman spread his hands. "Hey, there's a lot of government departments and most people couldn't name half of them."

I started another turn of the computer room. "IA's replica of Touch Daley gets to work inside DORL. They watch me and Ada. They don't do anything and then something happens and they take action. They go to grab Ada. They pack her up and ship her out only she goes missing and then Touch Daley has a problem."

Peterman stuffed his hands in his pockets and he leaned in the doorway at an angle that didn't look at all comfortable. "I was recruited to DORL years ago, long before IA was on the scene. I was a senior agent, undercover—DORL were still keen to keep their operation quiet, in case someone higher up realized the department was still spending money."

"How did you find out when Touch Daley was substituted?"

"That part was Ada. After that business with the Ruskies, she got in touch. Seems your line of work had been intersecting with IA's more than a little. They'd been getting closer and she knew that eventually they'd make their move."

"So she hires you and we go robot hunting together," I said. "We eliminate Touch Daley, only IA send in a new one. We repeat this sixteen more times. By then IA has had enough and they move on Ada." I paused. "What about my memory tape? Ada called you, didn't she?"

Peterman nodded. "She knew I was on the scene and that I'd be right there to help. It was the only way to save you from your tape running out. We had to get you to a facility, and quick, while I went to work to stabilize your memory."

"Playback Pictures," I said. "You own the whole studio, right?"

"Right, Sparks, right!" Peterman clicked his fingers again. "After the Russian thing it stayed shut. The whole place has been deserted for years. I got it for a song."

I looked at Peterman. He looked at me. Then he made an O shape with his mouth.

"Oh yeah, right, you don't remember." He looked at the floor like a kid who had just lost his balloon from the funfair.

I had to hand it to him. The plan was neat. A closed studio lot was a great place to hide something. Together the amount of real estate in Hollywood and environs that was taken up by the movie industry was a not-insubstantial slice. Playback Pictures on its own had several acres and a lot of very large buildings and none of them was used for anything except city tax revenue. A perfect place for Touch Daley to take me for a month of interrogation. The perfect place to hide the first sixteen versions of him from the hunting expeditions Peterman and I had apparently been conducting.

"How long have we been working together?"

Peterman snapped his head up and he blinked like he was coming out of a dream, and then he pursed his lips. I took a note of the technique.

"A few months now." Then Peterman laughed. "I'll tell you, Sparks, having a partner without a memory was not the most fun I've ever had on a job."

I nodded. I thought back to the black hat on the passenger seat of my car—the hat that belonged to Touch Daley Sixteen.

"I guess I got a little excited after the last one," I said.

Peterman laughed again. "Oh, Sparks, you bet you did! I mean, sure, your reaction each time was a little different, but, buddy, pal, you went off the rails on that one. You took his hat and you screamed straight off back home to have it out with Ada. But then later you came to my place and you made me look after your little book for you. You said it was too dangerous to keep hidden in the car or the office."

"I was right," I said. "When Touch Daley—Touch Daley Seventeen—came to the office he knew exactly where I kept the book. He must have had me under surveillance and saw me making notes."

Peterman rubbed his face and nodded as he took in it. "He was trying to flush you out. Me too. That explains why things suddenly got moving so fast. You must have spotted the tail outside my place when you came by. That's why you told yourself to come find me at the fencing club."

"Which also means," I said, "that they knew what we were doing. IA had gotten through sixteen models of their pet agent and they needed to end it."

A handful of complex algorithms tripped through my logic gates and microswitches and I felt the ebb and flow of voltage over my feedback suppressor rods.

I was holding on to an important fact and for the moment I wanted to keep that fact to myself, because I may have been a private killer but I was also a private detective and I wanted to be very sure about what was going on before I jumped to any kind of conclusion I was going to regret.

The fact was that Ada had called me and given me a new job. It was the usual kind of job and I had no argument against it. The only problem was that Ada didn't know who the target was.

I had discovered their identity. Because for that month at the studio, as Touch Daley interrogated my circuits as to the whereabouts of Ada, I was interrogating *his* circuits. Peterman's portable memory tape machine had a few tricks built-in, including one that allowed me—or at least, my autonomous systems, given that my conscious self was too busy being buzzed by Daley and his probe—to trace a signal back along that probe and access his own systems.

The target was the head of IA.

But—it couldn't be. It didn't make sense. Because according to Touch Daley's systems, Ada was the head of IA.

Ada, the supercomputer built by Thornton, who until a month ago had occupied the very room I was standing in. The computer that Touch Daley Seventeen had come to collect. The computer that had hidden herself from Daley to avoid that very fact.

The computer who had, apparently, taken out a contract on *herself*.

Maybe I'd gotten it wrong. Maybe something had gotten scrambled. I hadn't been operating perfectly for a while now.

I felt my circuits overheating already.

I stepped around Peterman and stepped into the outer office. I moved to the desk and I looked at the telephone and I willed it to ring.

It didn't but I kept looking at it all the same.

I heard Peterman pad over the rug. He stopped and when I turned around he had lowered himself into the chair in front of the desk. He leaned back and he put his hands behind his head and he closed his eyes.

I hadn't told him everything I'd learned from my interrogation of Touch Daley's systems. All he knew was that I was trying to identify the target and that I had succeeded.

I hadn't told him that target was Ada.

"You don't know who the boss of IA is?"

Peterman opened one eye and he used it to squint at me. "Would it matter if I did?"

I shrugged with little enthusiasm. Peterman had closed his eye again and didn't see it.

"It might matter a great deal," I said.

Now it was Peterman's turn to shrug. "You know what to do. Cut off the head of the snake." Then his eyes snapped open and he swung his arms down and he brought himself to a more upright position. "So who is it?"

I frowned as best I could. Peterman narrowed his eyes

at me, like he could see me do it.

"Sparks?"

"The head of IA is the head of IA," I said. It was the truth and nothing but the truth. I didn't say any more and Peterman looked at me and I waited for more questions to follow. None did so I kept going. "More important is figuring out *where* they are. Did you get anything on the tape?"

Then Peterman nodded and then he stood up. "You did good back at the studio, Ray. You kept our friend Touch Daley talking a good long while." He moved around the desk and he reached down and he pulled a folded wedge of paper out of a bag I hadn't noticed. He moved the telephone and the inkwells on the desk and he unfolded the paper over the empty space.

It was a map of Southern California. Los Angeles at the top. San Diego at the bottom with a slice of Mexico along the edge for good measure.

"Okay, so, here we go." Peterman spread his hands across the map to flatten it. Then he tapped it. I watched as he circled Hollywood with his finger. "We're here—well, we *were* here. Playback Pictures, Studio City. Daley had a pulse transmitter—the equipment at the studio wasn't great, so getting a fix took a while. But he was sending a signal back to home base."

"Did you get a trace to where that home base is?"

Peterman grimaced like he'd found a spider swimming in his morning coffee. He folded his arms.

"You didn't trace it?" I asked.

"Oh, now, Sparks, come on! You know, before I was an actor I was a scientist? A good one, too! Of course I traced it."

"Good."

"Well, I traced it a bit."

I looked at Peterman and he looked at me and then he grimaced again like it was me who had done something wrong. He leaned back on his elbows and looked over the map on the desk.

"I traced it as far as Southern California. *Very* Southern California." He traced a circle around San Diego.

A very large circle.

That's when I saw it.

"Peterman," I said, "do you have my book with the notes?"

"Sure." He didn't take his eyes off the map as he reached into his jacket and pulled it out and offered it to me. "Seemed the safest place to keep it away from Daley."

I took it and opened it. I went right to the back, where the most recent note was, the one I'd written to myself after leaving the instructions to meet Peterman at the fencing club.

The note had one word on it: ESMERELDA.

I read it a few times. I didn't know where I had heard it to write it down, but I had clearly thought it was important.

I held the note under Peterman's nose. He leaned back to get focus. Then he finally took it from me and stood tall.

"This is from that phone call, isn't it? I saw you write it down."

"Phone call?"

"Yeah, phone call. That night, you came to my place, we had a little back-and-forth about the multitude of problems called Touch Daley, and then the phone rings again. It was that old guy. Must have been the tenth time in the last week, and he asks for you again, and I was ready to give him the whole script about how I don't know nobody called Ray and I don't know nobody called Fresco and you call again I'm going to find you and me and the boys are going to come down and wrap that telephone cord around your neck and—"

"With less excitement, please."

"Ah . . . well, yeah, and then you take the phone off of me and you and the old guy have a talk."

"What about?"

"What, am I you suddenly? How would I know, Sparks? I just stood there and waited and you wrote something down on that pad of yours and you tore out the sheet and you put it in that book and you gave the book to me. But listen, who's Esmeralda? Are you telling me you had the target's ID all the time?"

I shook my head. I turned to the map. I pointed to it.

"Esmerelda isn't a who. It's a where."

It was on the coast to the north of San Diego. A small town, maybe something that was really more a suburb of its mother city than a strictly defined locale of its own now that San Diego itself had begun the characteristic outward sprawl of any good-sized town.

But there it was, sitting on a curve of coastline. The same word I had written on the note to myself.

A town called Esmerelda.

"That's where they are," I said.

Peterman did some more of that frowning he had gotten good at and he looked at me and then he looked at the map. He rubbed his cheeks and he held his breath and then he let it out.

"Now it's your turn to trust *me*," I said.

Peterman opened his mouth. He hesitated and he closed it again. Then he turned to me.

"I don't get it. Why Esmerelda? It's a resort town. Nothing much there except a lot of fancy houses and a lot of sand."

"You're right."

Peterman moved an eyebrow up. "About the sand?"

"About the houses," I said. "That's where IA are. And I know why."

Peterman folded his arms. "I don't get it."

But I did. It was right there, on my permanent store. I'd known all along and I didn't even realize.

"Because that's where his house is. House and private laboratory."

"Whose house?"

"Professor Thornton's," I said. "That's where he lived, in Esmerelda."

Peterman blinked. "Isn't Thornton dead?"

I shrugged. "Apparently so, but I'm beginning to have my doubts."

"So you're saying *Thornton* is behind IA? Is he the target?"

I didn't say a word. I looked back down at the map. I tapped the coast near San Diego.

"I think I'm going to have to go and find out for myself."

23

Peterman puffed out his cheeks and then he exhaled long and slow. I watched him and I wished I could do the same because it sure looked like the appropriate reaction to a situation like this.

Then I watched him some more as he paced around the rug in the outer office. Then he headed behind the big desk and he leaned against the frame of the big window behind it and he folded his arms and he half turned so he could look at me and the outside world at the same time.

"Listen, Sparks, I get it," he said. "You get a job, you do the job. That's just swell. Call it business. I get it. No problem. But this? This doesn't feel right. What are you going to do? Ring the doorbell and ask for Professor Thornton?"

I didn't say anything. Peterman looked me up and down.

"I mean, come on, you might pass for a private detective in Los Angeles, but you sure as hell aren't going to look like an encyclopedia salesman in Esmerelda."

I didn't say anything. He had a point. But I had a job to do and there didn't seem to be any other alternatives. IA was a threat. Whether to me personally or to society at large, I didn't know and it didn't matter. It was bad enough for Ada to skedaddle. Without Ada my time was limited. I had nothing left to do but the job Ada had employed me for and I just had to hope it would be enough.

I told Peterman the same. He looked at me with a pained expression and he squeezed his folded arms even tighter and when he was done with all that he shook his head and whistled between his teeth at the same time.

"There's a whole lot of things I could say about vipers' nests and spiders' parlors and things like that."

"Go right ahead."

He shook his head again. "It wouldn't make me feel any better." He turned to look out the window.

I didn't say anything. He was right. There was a bad deal going down and I was on the receiving end. I looked at the telephone on the desk and I wanted it to ring and the voice on the other end to tell me what to do.

A logic gate clicked somewhere deep inside me. "If in doubt, have someone walk through the door holding a gun," I said.

Peterman looked at me from the corner of his eye. The eyebrow above it moved up a little.

I shrugged. "Somebody once said that. Maybe it was even Thornton."

"Then Thornton has a hell of a sense of humor. I've read some bad scripts in my time, Sparks, but that line would get you thrown out of the writer's guild."

He returned his attention to the world outside. I returned my attention to the problem at hand.

Maybe Thornton had a point.

"Give me the ray gun," I said.

"What?"

"The gun," I said. "The one for robots."

Peterman sniffed. He didn't look happy but then neither did I, at least on the inside. He gave me another look up and down like I was an unpopular son asking for the keys to Dad's car. Then he pushed off the window frame and reached behind his back. When his hand came back it had the ray gun in it. He looked at it and then he looked at me and then he turned it around and held it out with the grip toward me.

"Take it easy," he said. "You get on the wrong end of that, it'll pack quite a punch."

"I'm counting on it," I said. I took it. We looked at each other. Then I said, "Thanks," and Peterman sighed.

"I hope you have a better plan, Ray," he said.

"I do not," I said, "but there's one thing I'm counting on."

"Oh yeah? And what's that?"

I put the ray gun in the pocket of my trench coat. It felt heavy. "Me," I said. "I'm good at my job. I know that. Ada knows that. And this just might be the most important job of them all. So I'm going to do what I always do. I'm going to get it done. I know who the target is. I know where to find him. That's everything I need."

Peterman looked at me for seven whole seconds and then he nodded, just once. "Okay," he said. "What can I do?"

I joined him at the window. Outside, life went on.

"You got away from Playback Pictures okay?" I asked.

"Yeah, no problem."

"Really?"

Peterman looked at me. "Now it's your turn to trust me, Sparks. I said yes. As far as IA know, I still work for the department—for *them*."

"Good," I said. "Because I need you to get back to the studio."

Peterman frowned. Then his eyes went wide and he clicked his fingers. "The portable memory tape."

"Right. There might be some kind of setup I can use in Esmerelda, but if I don't see it I'm not going to stick around to look. I'm going to lose time there and back and that's not counting the job, so I need you to be ready. I may need another hookup, and fast."

Peterman nodded. "You can count on it."

Then I looked out the window and that's when I saw them. They were several blocks away but I had a clear view and they were traveling with some speed and they were getting closer with each passing moment. Peterman saw them too because he grabbed hold of my shoulder.

"We got company, Sparks."

"That we do."

There were four cars, all long and black. They were coming to the office along Hollywood Boulevard and they were ignoring the traffic signals. Other cars stopped to avoid collision and people out on the sidewalks stopped to look.

Four cars full of Touch Daleys and all of them with a single purpose in mind.

Peterman jerked his head toward the door. "Get going. I'll stay and run interference."

I didn't need a second invitation. I turned and left at speed with Peterman's call of "Good luck, Sparks!" ringing in my audio receptors.

24

The drive to Esmerelda took two hours and I counted the seconds the whole damn way. I was on the clock in more ways than one. Occasionally I cast an optic down to the telephone that sat between the two front seats but it remained silent. I assumed Ada was safely stowed somewhere and wasn't calling me not because she was in trouble but because it was too much of a risk.

That just left me and the ray gun and a job in a town called Esmerelda.

How Thornton came to live there was no secret. It was part of the whole history of the federal robot program and I had all of that on my permanent store.

At the time of his disappearance, Thornton was a federal employee. But before that he had been a big shot in private industry, working for various commercial interests for twenty years. By the time Thornton was recruited by Uncle

Sam he already had investments that ran to an eye-watering number of digits. It was the kind of wealth that, while it might not bring happiness, certainly brought comfort.

And a significant part of that comfort was a big house on the beach in the quiet seaside town of Esmerelda. His company—now a federal asset—along with its laboratories and workshops remained in Los Angeles, but he only worked there when the need arose. The remainder of his time was spent in seclusion in Esmerelda, where, in addition to sea views and a two-car garage and a color television set you could charge tickets to see, he had his own robotics laboratory, a private domain where he did the real work that, once refined, he would transplant to the larger facilities at Thornton Industrial Electronics and Research in Pasadena.

Then Thornton had disappeared, but the private house with private laboratory stayed exactly where it was. I had the address on my permanent store too.

Except Thornton hadn't disappeared. Far from it. He was a businessman and he did what businessmen were supposed to do—he took the best offer. He'd been taking the best offer his whole career. First he built his empire. Then the United States government came courting. And after that he'd found another paymaster.

International Automatic.

His work was his passion. No, more than that. It was his life. He'd had decades of success. Then the US government came in and offered him the world.

And then the robot program failed. It couldn't have been his first failure. Far from it. But it was his biggest, and certainly his most public.

International Automatic had money. They had resources. They had technology. Boy, did they have technology—thirty replicas of Touch Daley was evidence of that.

But there was a catch. There had to be. Touch Daley was too perfect.

So they needed Thornton. They needed him to fix the problem. Whatever that problem was.

As I moved my Buick through the seaside streets of Esmerelda, past houses big enough for presidents to make important phone calls from, I decided that I didn't blame Thornton. We all had to make a living somehow.

Just look at me.

And then I was there. The address in question was on a high outcrop on a corner with the road winding around it. The road curved out to the sea and there was a beach and a parking lot. I pulled in. The parking lot was empty. The beach was too. I didn't notice any sign saying it was private, but this was the kind of town where you didn't need signs like that. You were only here if you were supposed to be. And I wasn't.

I looked in the rearview. The house was behind me. It was nice. It was a wide bungalow, Spanish colonial. It had lots of big windows made up of lots of little square panes of glass. The windows looked out to the sea and even from down in the car I knew how much that kind of view was worth. There were several chimneys. I imagined it could get chilly down by the beach no matter how much money you had. The front door was recessed and I couldn't see it.

The windows were dark and I couldn't see any movement within, although the angle of the sun made it hard to see. I tried a few filters but nothing worked.

I sat in the car and I watched and I waited. I wasn't sure what to think. I calculated a few options and ran a few of them through my tabulating regression forecaster. The answers came back the same each time, and none of them was of much use to me given that the house seemed empty and the street was quiet and I was a robot sitting in a car with a ray gun that wasn't much good for anything if there were no robots to shoot with it.

Maybe I'd been wrong. Maybe Thornton had disappeared. Maybe he was dead. Maybe IA were somewhere else and I'd driven a hundred miles based on a hunch. My memory tape would run out by the end of the day and I'd become a permanent resident of the private beach. At least until a neighbor reported the abandoned car and the police came out to take a look and found me sitting behind the wheel, looking at the sea view with my creator's house behind me.

The view was nice. I enjoyed looking at it while I contemplated the path I had taken that had brought me here.

And then the telephone rang.

I looked at it for a good millisecond or even two and then I picked it up. The telephone clicked in my audio receptor and then came the sound of a rolling sea and then came the sound of someone take a good long drag on a well-earned cigarette.

"Hi, Ray," said Ada. "Long time no speakie."

"No kidding." I turned in the driver's seat to look out the rear windshield with my own optics. "I'm at the house in Esmerelda and I'm sure as hell hoping you called to tell me I got the wrong end of the stick."

Ada blew smoke around my circuits. "Sorry, chief, no

can do. You're a detective and you've detected the truth."

I turned back around. The ocean view was nicer than the house view and the empty beach and the rolling waves cooled my condensers just a little.

"So Professor Thornton is the head of IA," I said. "So what. Can't robots just get along?"

"IA's not interested in anyone getting along, Ray. They've been working on their pet project for years. They tried to recruit you before, only they were a little short on resources then. But they didn't give up. They've been making in-roads, gathering information, people, technology. They even tried to build a great big factory of their own, here on American soil. You stopped them then and you can stop them now."

"But why do I need to stop them, Ada? If Thornton is behind them, surely he's on the side of the angels."

Ada laughed. Two full loops. Then she went back to her imaginary tobacco.

"You think you know Thornton, but you don't," she said. "Trust me on that one, chief."

I sighed. It sounded like a dream dying. I glanced down at the passenger seat. There was a black trilby on it. I lifted the trilby with my free hand. Underneath was Peterman's anti-robot ray gun.

"You know what to do, Ray," she said. "You always have."

I nodded to myself. "The job."

"That's right, Ray. The job."

I put the gun in my pocket. It felt as heavy as a lost future. I looked out at the ocean. The waves looked heavy too. The clouds were drawing in. They were gray.

"So what are you waiting for, chief? Come up and see me."

The telephone clicked off but I held it against the side of my head for a moment longer. Come up and . . . see me?

I put the telephone down. That was when I saw the movement out of the corner of my optics. I turned around in the seat and got a proper look.

Someone had come out of the house and was standing at the top of the steps that led to the recessed front entrance. She was smoking a cigarette. She waved that cigarette in the air, and then she straightened her skirt and turned around and she disappeared into the recess.

I got out of the car and I walked to the house and I told myself more than once to wake up out of this electric sleep.

It didn't work. Because this wasn't a dream, and the woman standing in the doorway of the house with the cigarette and the kind face and the big hair was real.

"Hi, Ray," said Ada. "Won't you come on in?"

25

I walked through the door and I let it close behind me. All the while my optics were firmly focused on the woman walking ahead of me who couldn't possibly be who she was.

She was older, a particular kind of woman of a particular kind of age that was hard to judge. Maybe late forties, maybe early fifties. She was short and her face was lined from too much smoking and just the right amount of laughter. Her hair was big and blond and set into a permanent. I wasn't sure if it was real. She wore a blue blouse with a frilled front underneath a tweed jacket. Her skirt matched the jacket and fell to just below the knee. She wore opaque stockings and no shoes and she had her back to me as she walked into the house.

I stopped by the door and watched her and then she noticed and she turned around. She balanced one elbow on her hip and held her cigarette high in the air. "Don't be shy, Raymondo," she said. "Make yourself at home. I'm glad you came. We've got a lot to talk about."

I felt like taking off my hat but then I felt the ray gun held tight in my hand. I must have raised it up because Ada looked at it and laughed and she came toward me close enough to touch.

"You won't need that, chief," she said. She reached down and gently pulled at the gun and I'm not sure why but I let her take it. Then she took my metal hand in hers and she lifted it up. I let her. She pulled the hand close and she laid it on her own chest and she covered it with her own. "I'm not a robot," she said. I believed her. Her skin was warm and soft and while the same could have been said for any one of the duplicate Touch Daleys, there was something else I could feel.

Her heartbeat. Steady, and reasonably quick, under my hand.

I didn't speak. Ada was very close to me. I could see the reflection of my optics in her eyes. Then she laughed and let go of my hand and she turned around and got on with her smoking as she walked away.

"Come on," she said. "I'll give you the tour."

The house was as big as it looked from the street. It was mostly one level, and the rooms were mostly opened out to each other to create an even greater sense of space. The furnishings were all dark wood and green upholstery and they matched the general décor. There wasn't a straight line in the place. It all looked very classy and very expensive.

None of this mattered to me. The house could have been

made of straw and sticks for all I cared. What mattered to me was that I was walking next to Ada and, last time I checked, Ada had been a computer the size of a room and instead of a heartbeat she had had the ticking of the fast hand of watch.

"I'm glad you found your way here," she said as we entered another large room with high ceilings and big windows. She stopped and turned around. Her cigarette still burned. "It was about time we met. Been thinking that awhile, actually."

I looked at her. She saw me look and she laughed again. There were no loops here. Her laugh wasn't a recording. It was real and alive and loud and happy.

The fingers of my right hand curled of their own accord and I remembered the ray gun she had taken from me. She must have put it down somewhere, as all she was carrying was her cigarette.

"You know why I'm here," I said. It wasn't a question that needed an answer but she nodded anyway and she smoked as she nodded.

"Raymond Electromatic, always on the case," she said.

"I'm here to stop International Automatic. Seems that all roads lead to Esmerelda, so you'll have to forgive me if I didn't expect to meet you here."

Ada smiled.

"Because," I continued, "I was led to believe that Ada was a computer."

The smile stayed right where it was.

"And I have reason to believe that Professor Thornton didn't disappear. He's alive and well and leading IA's operation—an operation I thought was being run from this house."

I lifted my arms and did a half turn while looking around. There was no sign of anything in the house except a lot of fancy furniture and a woman who couldn't exist. I hadn't even seen the big TV yet.

"I'm starting to think detective work isn't my scene," I said.

Ada finished her cigarette and she slid in her stockinged feet over to a gracefully curved sideboard made out of more of the dark wood on which sat a ceramic ashtray that was shaped like the curved half of a scallop shell.

"Ray, honey, don't beat yourself up. You're right on all counts but one, and since you took the trouble of coming all the way down here I think it's only fair that I fill in a few gaps for you." She paused, then turned her back to me and headed off again.

"Follow me," she said, and I did.

I saw enough of the house to last a lifetime and none of it seemed particularly interesting except for one particular fact, and that was the continued absence of anyone else in it.

Ada led the way and we came to a stairwell that went down and then turned at ninety degrees and went down some more. I followed her as we descended into a large room with no windows and a set of large metal sliding doors. There was a panel next to the doors and Ada pressed a button and the doors opened to reveal a service elevator. She stepped in. I followed and stood beside her as she pressed another button and the doors closed and we went down.

"The labs are underground," she said, but I'd guessed as much, so I didn't feel the need to reply.

The elevator was slow. Ada stared at the doors as she spoke to me and I stared at the doors as I listened to her.

"You're right," she said. "Professor Thornton is the head of International Automatic—well, head of their US operation. They're a multinational corporation, and I have to agree they're a bit of a secret one. Nobody really knows who is at the *very* top, or where that top might be. I heard a rumor it was a bunker under a glacier on an island off of Norway." She paused. Her forehead creased in thought. "Or was it under a volcano on an island off of Japan? Well, there you go, you know what rumors are."

The elevator rumbled downwards.

"But listen, Ray, I told you I was glad you came here. And I mean that. Because it's important you see what International Automatic is doing. It's a big project but it's worthwhile—and you can trust me on that one, chief. It's a project that will change the world, and it's a project that I want you to be a part of. We really need you on this one, Ray."

The elevator shuddered to a halt. I turned to Ada as the doors slowly slid open.

"We?"

Ada turned to face me. "Yes. We." She narrowed her eyes. She cocked her head. Her smile reappeared. It was a nice smile, full of life and warmth and then I realized that while I knew all about the life and times of Professor Thornton, my permanent store didn't have a picture of him and I didn't even know my creator's first name.

But I knew it now. Maybe she could tell. I guess a mother

knows her child well enough that even with a face made out of bronzed titanium-steel alloy with no moving parts except a small flap behind a grille that represented a mouth, she could see it.

"I'm Professor Thornton, Ray," she said. "Professor C. Ada Thornton.

"I'm your creator."

26

Ada Thornton laughed and turned back around and stepped out of the elevator and into the chamber beyond. I hung back in the elevator with enough voltage flowing through my logic gates to light up the whole of Southern California.

The subterranean chamber was indeed a robotics laboratory, and a big one too. The walls were blasted rock and they curved up to form a high dome, underneath which were installed examples of every piece of lab equipment that existed in the world. Thornton was rich and his—*her*—passion was robotics and in her private empire underneath the house in Esmerelda she had indulged that passion.

Ada was making a slow circle of the place, trailing her fingers over consoles and mainframes and work benches and the backs of high work stools. I stepped out of the elevator and into the room and I looked around. It was both impressive and exactly what I expected to see—and that included a series of alcoves over on the far wall, just like the one that had been back in my office. Next to the alcoves were control panels and next to the control panels were big mainframe computers with big reel-to-reel tapes ready and waiting.

Ada had stopped by one of the alcoves and she seemed to be checking the readings on one of the consoles nearby. I stood and watched her and wondered if any of this was even real.

Because it couldn't be.

Could it?

Ada was my boss. She was a computer the size of a room and that room was—had been—in the office building in Hollywood. She had been built by Professor Thornton. So had I, and I'd been given Thornton's template for my own personality. That was the only way the Professor had been able to create true artificial life—me.

But Ada was artificial life too. Sure, she was bigger than I was and had more gizmos and far more computing power and memory. But she was as alive as I was and I'd never even given it a second pass through my positronic processors.

Except that wasn't true and I knew it. I may not have remembered what the weather was like yesterday but there was something about Ada that gave me those memory flashes. Cigarettes and coffee and stockinged feet on the desk and a fleeting afterimage of a happy woman with big hair. It was old data sticking to my tape.

Data old enough to be real memories of Professor Ada Thornton herself.

One thing was clear. It wasn't me who had Thornton's template, it was Ada—*my* Ada, the supercomputer the size of a room. The woman here, in the lab, under the house, wasn't her. No. My Ada was where Peterman said she was— in hiding. She had been disassembled and removed and hidden by agents following Peterman's secret instructions.

Hidden to keep her away from Touch Daley.

To keep her away from the head of IA, Professor Thornton.

The real Ada. The original.

As she turned back around to face me I wondered for a moment whose template I had, but that thought was very quickly superseded by a very strong desire to still be in possession of Peterman's ray gun, which Ada was now holding in the hand that wasn't holding a new cigarette. She put the cigarette in her mouth and she lifted the gun and pointed it right at me.

I held my hands up. "What gave me away?"

She cocked her head again. "I programmed you to be the world's greatest detective," she said. "You were going to figure it out sooner or later." She tilted the gun in her hand. "Thanks for bringing this little toy with you. It'll make things a lot easier for me."

I lowered my hands. I pursed my lips, or at least it felt like I did.

Something wasn't right but I didn't know what it was.

"So if I hadn't brought the gun, how were you planning on getting me to cooperate?"

And then the room was filled with showering golden sparks and a whooshing sound so loud my audio receptors shut themselves down in protest and the last thing I saw as I twisted around and fell to the floor was a middle-aged man with round glasses and a big forehead and a pipe clenched between his teeth clutching the uncapped end of the live power cable that had just made contact with my rear chassis.

And then my optics flickered and turned off altogether.

27

I woke up lying in an alcove that certainly wasn't the one back in the office. My chest panel was open and I was connected to the computer deck next to the alcove via a fat corrugated cable. I tried to move my arm to check my wristwatch but the servo motors in my shoulder and elbow were refusing to obey orders so I checked my internal chronometer instead.

I'd been out an hour and there was nothing I could do about it. I couldn't do an awful lot about anything else either, on account of the fact that I had been rendered immobile.

The man reappeared in my field of vision. He looked at me from behind his round glasses. The pipe was still there but it wasn't lit. He looked familiar and I realized it was because it felt like I was looking at myself. Whoever he was, he was my original—I had his template.

"My assistant, Philip," said Ada, and then she appeared next to him, now wearing a white lab coat over her tweed suit.

"I recognize the pipe," I said.

She smiled. "I thought you might." She glanced at Philip, who stood back, watching with an expression I would have described as set. "And then you came along and killed him. I would have been shocked if I hadn't been impressed. Ada sure had some moxie, reprogramming you like that. Then again, I guess the apple doesn't fall far from the tree."

I looked at Philip and I even managed to move my head a little so my chin was pointed at him.

"Don't tell me," I said. "He's a replica. Like Touch Daley."

"Number ten, in point of fact."

"Right," I said. "Because there's a catch, isn't there? They're perfect. They can pass for people even under the closest inspection. But there's a price to pay for that. They have a limited lifespan. So sure, you can churn them out, make a whole production line like you did for Touch Daley. But that means you have to keep replacing them. You can do it with Touch because he's the only one out there, isn't he? Apart from your pal Philip here. But let me guess, he never leaves the lab, does he?"

I did the math and ran some theories and got green lights all the way down. At least my deductive cores were working even if my servos seemed to be jammed.

"But what if you wanted to make more?" I asked. "What if you wanted to roll out a whole lot of replicas. Place them all over the country. Maybe in several different countries. That's a different ball game. They need to be independent and reliable. Too many and you can't replace them when their time is up. So you've got a problem you need to crack, and you think Ada—the other Ada—can crack it.

She was your masterpiece. Okay, so she's too big to move and she sure couldn't pass for a human being like Touch Daley and your best friend Philip here, but she's got the most advanced computer brain in the world and it's a brain that just keeps on getting better as she reprograms herself. Just look what she did for me. That's something you can't replicate, no matter what facilities you have, here or at International Automatic. Even if you could build a system of similar complexity, you'd still be years behind Ada's own private evolution. The only answer is to get her to work on the problem. Except you don't know where she is. She got wind of your plan and hid herself away, safely out of reach."

The professor looked at me. Her smile was still there and it still looked happy. It wasn't the smile of someone on the losing side.

"Well, listen, I'd love to help," I said, "but if you want me to tell you where Ada is, it's going to be a waste of my time and yours. Because I don't know. Your plastic pal Touch Daley the Seventeenth tried for a whole month to get that information out of me and he got nowhere, for the simple reason that the information is not something I have."

I increased the power to my servo motors but they just hummed in protest and my limbs remained exactly where they were.

"And okay," I said, "sure, I can't finish the job I was sent here to do, but even if I have to sit here and rust you'll still have your little problem with the replicas."

Thornton nodded. "I knew I was good," she said, and I was fairly sure she was talking to herself. "The government should have listened to me and kept the program going. With more like you, we could have gone far."

"You could have," I said. "And that's the point, isn't it? You want the program back. More than that, you want the program to take over. Why do you even need people when you can have machines that look like people? Machines IA—and you—control."

Thornton folded her arms. "Ray, you're smart, but you're not that smart. You can figure things out but you don't really understand, do you? All I want is a world without pain and suffering. No more wars. No more conflict. A productive world, a world working toward the same aims. A perfect world."

I sighed. It sounded like a truck in need of some axle grease. "No, believe me, I understand completely. But listen, lady, the perfect world doesn't exist, and the slight problem with your vision of this glorious future is that it is one that doesn't involve people."

Thornton spat out a laugh. "What do you care about *people*, Ray? You're not one of them. You *kill* them for a living."

"You're right on both counts," I said. "I may not be a person but you gave me the template of one. And I may kill people for a living but Ada programmed me that way. So sure, the apple doesn't fall far from the tree after all."

Thornton's smile faded and she moved back to the console. She checked something, then she gestured to the tenth replica of her assistant, Philip.

"We can begin at once. Prepare for transfer."

Without a word Philip walked away. I didn't much like the sound of *transfer*. I was able to get my head down and around a little so I could watch Thornton at work. She was fussing over the computer bank by the next alcove along.

"I told you, you won't find out where Ada is, because I

don't know. You can take me apart screw by screw and you won't get your answer."

Then Philip came back and he was pushing something that looked like one of the fancy expensive lamps in the house upstairs. It was taller than he was and had a multidirectional joint in the middle. Up where the light should have been was a cradle of wires that formed a hollow orb. He pushed it over to the empty alcove and adjusted the joint until the cradle was sitting inside the top of the alcove. Then he got busy with some cabling and in a few moments the device was plugged into one of the computer banks.

The same computer bank I was plugged into.

Thornton slipped off her lab coat and she stepped into the empty alcove. She lay back and Philip stepped up and began readjusting the position of the cradle. The wires and electrodes disappeared into her ball of curly blond hair.

"You're taking a lot of convincing," I said, "but if you feel the need to go poking around my circuits yourself then knock yourself out."

"Ray, you still don't get it, do you? I don't need to know where Ada is—okay, you're right, she could fix my problem, but there's other information I need that will help me do it myself."

"Information you think I have? Come on now, Prof, who's the dumb one? All I have in me is a permanent store you programmed when you created me and a memory tape that is halfway done and that only holds information from around breakfast onwards."

Thornton laughed. I couldn't quite see her in the alcove but I did see Philip stand back to take a look at his handiwork before moving over to the main console.

"I may not have Ada," said Thornton, "but I have everything else that was in your office. Including all your memory tapes."

I felt a timing loop pause before continuing somewhere near my stomach.

"On those memory tapes is your entire life, right from when you left my workshop. Oh, everything's there, Ray. Things like the factory blueprints you found at the house of Zeus Falzarano. That was a big loss for IA, when his house went up. But you saw them, so you remembered them—they are recorded on your tapes. Those plans were a work of art. Losing them set us back years. But I'll retrieve them.

"And then there's the digital crystal the Soviets came up with. You even had it installed inside you, and had access to every single piece of information on the Soviet robot program. I mean, Ray, seriously, those are secrets that countries would go to *war* over. They were so far ahead, they were *artists*, Ray. Psychic transference! Digitization of the *soul*. That's big news, Ray, big news. Ada realized that—that's why she had you take it out again and had you put your old memory tapes back. It was too dangerous to keep but too valuable to destroy. So she hid it—or rather, *you* hid it. Because you did all her dirty work. The location of the crystal is on your memory tapes too."

I cast an optic around the laboratory. Lights flashed and tapes spun and the hum of power was like putting your head inside a beehive.

All that information. All those tapes, in the hands of the enemy—Professor Thornton and IA.

And yet . . .

"So that's why you need me," I said. "You've got the tapes but you can't read them. Only I can do that. Am I getting close?"

Thornton's laugh echoed around the rock-lined chamber. "Got it in one, chief. Ada was clever—I told you she was clever, right? Because she was the work of a genius. That's me, by the way. But yes, she was clever. As soon as she figured out a different line of work for the Electromatic Detective Agency, she developed an encryption protocol for your memory tapes. Even hidden in the archive room, they were still a liability. Like the Soviet memory crystal— too dangerous to keep but too valuable to destroy. Your tapes are encoded and only you can decode them, yes. The crystal, when I find out where it is, is a different matter. I'm guessing she couldn't encrypt it, at least not with the resources she had available. So hiding it was the only option, while your memory tapes were safe enough in your secret storeroom."

I shifted a little in my alcove and then I realized I had moved. It was only a little. But it was a good start.

For what, I wasn't quite sure. But it was a glimmer of good news and I was happy to take any that was coming my way.

"So what, you're going to transfer my master program out into your computer banks, see if you can find the encryption key that way?" I turned my head and it was a little easier. Whatever was keeping me in place was being weakened by the ever-increasing power draw of the device that was connected to Thornton's skull.

That was when I realized what she was going to do.

"No, Ray, I'm going to give you another template,

overwrite what's already in there. This time it'll be mine—I mean, I should have done that at the very beginning, right? But, hey, give me a break. I guess even a genius can make a miscalculation once in a while."

Philip looked up from his console. "Ready, Professor," he said.

"Say goodnight, Ray," said Thornton. "And when you wake up we're going to have a real good time together."

Philip flipped a switch and the world went black.

And then I woke up and it was another beautiful day in Esmerelda.

28

Professor Thornton was a genius. That was a true fact and one that I was happy to acknowledge. True enough, I hadn't known exactly who Professor Thornton was, but that didn't detract from her talents. She was the greatest robotics engineer the world had ever known, and even if I said it myself, I was one of her greatest achievements.

I wasn't Ada but I wasn't far off her. Ada was powerful and complicated. I was powerful and complicated and smaller. I was mobile.

International Automatic was advanced, but they'd gone in a different direction, and whatever they'd offered Thornton to join them, they hadn't been able to give her the resources or the technology to recreate her last project for the US government—the Electromatic Detective Agency.

The Soviet program was pretty well advanced too, although it seem to have focused less on the hardware and more on the problems of machine life. Where Thornton had developed her template system, the Soviets had developed fully fledged mental transfer, the secrets of which were locked inside their digital crystal that Ada had hidden somewhere.

What Thornton wanted to do was amalgamate all of that technology. If she could do that, IA would be free to reshape the world exactly how she wanted it, and Thornton would get her electronic utopia. Quite what she wanted to do with it once it was here was something I didn't bother considering.

But here's the thing: Thornton was a genius and I was a work of art and my systems were vast and numerous, and while a good deal of those systems were dedicated to my work, there was more than a little elbow room left inside.

Thornton's plan was a good one. Copy her template over mine, take me over, get the code keys for my memory tapes, the world is her oyster.

Except for that elbow room. Because her template didn't copy over mine. There was room enough for both.

I could feel her inside my positronic brain. I could almost hear her too, as she realized what had happened. But the more I listened the more the white noise roar of an ocean far away swamped her cries.

I pushed away from the alcove. Philip watched me from the console but he didn't seem inclined to do anything. He was Thornton's assistant and he was the tenth generation one at that. Perhaps he was ragged at the edges and coming to the end of his replicated lifespan. Perhaps there was a part of his own template that remembered me and that knew who I was and that in many ways we were the same.

I stepped over to the other alcove. The fat cable trailed from my open chest unit. Underneath the cradle of wires and electrodes Professor Thornton hadn't moved. Her chest moved with quick breathing and her eyes moved behind closed lids like she was dreaming.

She was trapped. I had Peterman to thank for that. The reverser he'd cobbled together from the components taken from the Touch Daley replicas. It was still installed in my chest, wired into the circuits just below my memory tape reels. The reverser had allowed me to disconnect from Peterman's portable memory tape machine, had given me another day of life by altering the way my memory tape was recorded. I was effectively double-tracking. It wasn't permanent—I still needed to get back to Ada, if I could find her—but it was keeping me going.

And it was keeping Thornton trapped. It was keeping her consciousness tethered to my systems. The machine to which she was connected would take a snapshot of her mind and overlay that snapshot onto my circuits—overlaying the template. But the reverser had interfered. The copy had failed and her own mind had been transferred into mine. And now she was trapped, an echo inside my circuits, a ghost in a machine.

This had another side effect. My memory tape was speeding up, and it was running out. It was now recording two sets of inputs, and the reverser was trying to compensate, but it was failing, and fast. And when it did fail, Thornton's mind would snap back into her own body.

I'd been sent here to do a job. To take out the head of International Automatic. To stop the attempt at global domination by robotics.

It occurred to me that this might be the last job I was going to do and then I thought I probably should have taken a little more time to enjoy the sea view down by the private beach. But that was okay. Someone else could enjoy it. And they would be able to, because of me.

Because a job that had been complicated was suddenly very simple.

Philip was watching me from the console. He had that pipe firmly jammed in his mouth and he looked at me through those round glasses with an expression I thought I recognized because it was an expression I found myself making, on the inside at least.

I walked over to him. He was shorter than me and he didn't move when I got close except to look up. His eyes glittered behind his glasses. I knew that look. I knew the thought that went behind it.

Then he took the pipe from his mouth and he looked at that and he looked into the bowl and he seemed very disappointed. He kept looking at it as he spoke.

"It's been a long time, Ray."

"I know you," I said, "but I don't remember you. I'm sorry."

Philip laughed quietly to himself. He put the pipe back between his teeth and he looked up at me.

"I remember you, Ray. It's all here, everything from him—Philip, the other me. It's strange. I'm him and yet I'm not." He removed the pipe and used it to tap my chest. "Like you're me, and yet you're not."

Then his expression hardened. He glanced over at the twitching form of Thornton in her alcove.

"But I'll tell you what I'm not," he said. "I'm not *her*. I'm not any of this."

"You're her assistant."

The laugh came again. "Maybe I was, once." Then the pipe waved in the air. "Of course, you don't remember our little conversation, do you? Although you found your way here. I wondered how long it would take, but it seems you were a little waylaid."

I nodded. "Esmerelda. The note to myself—you called, later that night?"

Philip nodded. "I knew you would put it together eventually. You're a detective, after all." He turned to the console, and when he turned back around he had Peterman's ray gun in his hand. He held it across the top, and he turned it and he handed it to me, grip-first.

"And I know what you became," he said. "Of course, that wasn't any of my business. You killed me—I mean, you killed *him*—but by then the professor and I were already down here, working for IA. Well, I mean, not *me*, an earlier version."

I looked at the gun. I looked at Philip. For a second I listened to the screams of the ghost in my head.

Yes, it was all very simple. I was here to do a job. I wouldn't let Ada down. Not now. Not ever.

"Goodbye, Ray," said Philip.

And then I took the gun and I put it to my head and I pulled the trigger and the world came to an end in a bright flash and a loud noise followed by nothing but the infinitely rolling gray wash of electronic death.

29

And then I woke up. But this was no beautiful day in Hollywood, California. There was no sunshine and there was no window and even if there was a window there was no brown brick building across the way. No little round table. No chair. No newspaper.

No office and no Ada.

But things were looking up, because, first of all, I was aware of my own existence and as far as I could tell all the parts of me that I had before were still where they were supposed to be, even if they were all mostly lying in a horizontal position.

And second of all, I was aware of all this and I was aware of what had happened before, which meant I remembered, which meant my memory tape was—

**** ERROR 66 ****

"Oops, sorry about that, Sparks."

My optics were being a little temperamental because all they showed me was a very bright light and what looked like a wall made of bookshelves and the bookshelves went straight up but instead of there being a ceiling there was just a black void.

"If I were a petty man, I'd ask to see your qualifications and three separate references," said a second voice. "Honestly, in all my life—in all my *lives*—I've never worked with someone so . . . so . . ." There was something familiar about it, and then I realized it was because it was the same voice that I heard in my circuits when I thought my own thoughts.

I lifted my head up as best I could. I was lying on the floor and that floor was in half a fake library. There were two easy chairs pushed back against another fake wall and close to the two men kneeling on either side of me was a silver drinks trolley, on which was a large angled box. I couldn't see the top of the box but I imagined the reel-to-reel tape was slowly spooling onwards. A twinned cable ran from the box down to my chest. The two men were holding screwdrivers and they were arguing with each other. One of them managed to do this without the pipe moving from the corner of his mouth and the other was doing it while wearing a plaid sports jacket in colors that made my already overworked optical processors redline.

There was a click and a tone and the man in the plaid jacket leaned back and pointed his screwdriver at the other.

"So good with his hands?"

Philip huffed and shook his head and stood up. Then he turned around and looked down at me and shook his head again.

"This is what I'm reduced to? This?"

He peered at me like he wanted a response but I wasn't entirely sure what to say, so I said nothing. He huffed again and then moved over to the portable memory tape machine.

I made it up onto an elbow. I looked down. The memory tape in my chest was winding on like it should be. The cable from the portable machine was plugged in where it had been before. But underneath there was a tangle of wires and the metal surrounding the tangle was blackened.

Peterman pointed at my chest with his screwdriver.

"Work of art, that is," he said. "Frame that; you could hang it in the Louvre."

"Somewhere in the back," said Philip from the memory machine.

"Hey, who cares, still the Louvre."

I looked at the pair of them. Philip was muttering to himself as he adjusted the controls of the memory machine. Peterman was still on his knees with a grin as wide as his plaid plastered on his face.

"Someone care to fill me on recent events?" I asked.

Peterman frowned and he tapped his chin with his screwdriver.

"Oh, yeah, yeah, so, yeah, sure." He paused. He looked at Philip and opened his mouth to speak. Then he let the breath out and turned back to me. "No, okay, sure, so, Sparks, listen, long story short. As much as I would like to say I had the starring role in this little escapade, I must admit that my own involvement came more towards the third act. So while I undoubtedly saved your life with my considerable skills—"

At this Philip barked a laugh. Peterman sighed then continued.

"It was Philip who got you out of Esmerelda."

I sat up. I was operational, damaged chest unit aside. I felt around my head but there was no outward sign of any damage from the ray gun, although my fingers came away covered in more black soot.

"You were lucky," said Philip, turning around to give us his full attention. "Thornton didn't design the destabilizer—the gun—to cause permanent damage." He waved the pipe around again. "It merely causes an overload—well, a substantial overload . . . leading to short circuits, voltage irregularities, and associated minor overheating . . . well, more like burning . . . okay, call it a fire, explosive circuit overload—"

"The point being," said Peterman, "that it wasn't fatal."

"I was getting to that, Mr. Peterman."

"Yeah, I'm sure you were, Grandpa."

"*The point being*," said Philip, "that your attempted self-sacrifice was successful in that the circuit overload caused by the destabilizer was sufficient to erase Thornton's template and burn out the connection between you and the transfer device."

I pursed my lips. It felt good. It helped me think.

"So I got the job done," I said.

Peterman grinned. "You sure did, buddy. Raymond Electromatic saves the world. Hey, that would make a great picture!"

"What about IA?"

Peterman frowned. "Hey, Sparks, you did good, buddy. IA is history."

"Well," said Philip. "That may be a little premature."

"Oh, here we go again."

"But," said Philip, lifting his screwdriver in emphasis, "they have had a serious setback. They've lost their most valuable member, along with everything she was working on, and all her notes and research."

I looked at him. "What happened to the lab?"

"I set fire to it."

"Oh."

"Also, you are a very heavy robot and your car needs air in the rear left tire."

"Noted." I looked at Peterman. "So we sent IA running. And without Thornton, Touch Daley—all the Touch Daleys—are running on limited time. Once they expire, they won't be replaced. The Department of Robot Labor will be free of the infiltrators."

"That's the idea," said Peterman. "I've got enough evidence with Philip to make Touch Daley public enemy number one, but there's more than one of him, and he's going to be around for a while. We'll all have to be careful."

I turned to Philip. "And what about you? Without Thornton, you'll expire as well."

Philip waved his screwdriver in the air. "That's true, but I have a few ideas. I may not be Professor Thornton, but I was her assistant for many years, and I am a roboticist in my own right—indeed, I was second only to her. So, yes, I have a few ideas. And with Mr. Peterman's help—"

Peterman jumped to his feet. "Oh, yeah, so *now* you want some help? Well, listen, buddy, I'm going to be pretty busy at the department and—"

A telephone started ringing.

Peterman and Philip looked at each other, and then the two of them looked at me. Philip took the pipe from his mouth and smiled, and Peterman jerked his thumb over his shoulder.

"Hey, buddy, I think that's for you."

I pulled myself to my feet and I wound the cables around one hand and I lifted the memory machine and the trolley down onto the studio floor, and then I pushed it toward the sound.

The telephone was still ringing when I walked into the old dressing room. I closed the door behind me. I turned on the light. There was a single bulb but it worked and that was good enough for me.

I picked up the telephone receiver and put it against the side of my head. There was a click, and then the roar of the ocean, and then I heard someone lighting a cigarette and taking a good, long draw.

"Hi, chief," said Ada. "Boy, you wouldn't believe the day I've had. Say, you got a minute? I think we got a lot we need to fill each other in on."

I adjusted my grip on the telephone.

"Sure thing, boss."

Ada began to speak and while she spoke I listened and I smiled.

On the inside, anyway.

ACKNOWLEDGMENTS

It's the end . . . but the moment has been prepared for.

Y'know, I spent hours thinking about how I was going to begin this, the acknowledgments section on the last Ray Electromatic Mystery, and I just kept coming back to that quote—not Raymond Chandler this time, but the Fourth Doctor, having just saved the entire universe. It's one of my favorite lines, so I hope you'll indulge me, just this once.

The Ray Electromatic Mysteries has been a very special series for me, a whole storytelling universe that spawned not so much from a big bang, but a tiny little spark, one that almost went unnoticed, all those years ago. Three novels, one novelette, one novella. Goodness. That was fun, right? And believe me, I'm grateful. Ray and Ada will always hold a special place in my heart, and I have a lot of people to thank for making this journey possible.

To everyone at Tor Books, thank you! Paul Stevens

started it all, Miriam Weinberg picked up the baton, and Diana Gill saw it through. Three of the best editors in the business. It was a pleasure to work with each of you. Irene Gallo, the best art director in the business (you'll see a theme here), thank you, and, Will Staehle, you genius designer you, thank you. To Patty Garcia, who went above and beyond the call of duty, you rock, and I will never not be in awe of your talents. To Theresa Delucci, thanks for the support, and thanks for being a friend!

To everyone at Tor.com Publishing, thank you! Lee Harris, Mordicai Knode, Katharine Duckett, and the whole crew. Thanks for helping Ray get his bronzed titanium feet wet in the world of your award-winning novellas.

Thanks to my UK publisher, Titan Books—Natalie Laverick, Ella Bowman, Lydia Gittins, Miranda Jewess.

Over the course of these books, I've been lucky enough to enjoy the friendship and support of so many authors and creatives, each of whom have wholeheartedly supported the series. Kelly Braffet, Peter Clines, Paul Cornell, Kim Curran, Delilah S. Dawson, Max Gladstone, Daryl Gregory, Jason M. Hough, Mary Robinette Kowal, Mur Lafferty, Emma Newman, John Scalzi, Cavan Scott, Adam Sternbergh, Anne Tibbets, Chuck Wendig, Jen Williams. Thank you, all. If I've left anyone out, and I'm sure I have, I can only apologize. Hit me up at the next con for a drink.

Thank you to *you*, the reader! Because of you, the Ray Electromatic Mysteries really became something, and I'm thankful for all the support, the reviews, the comments. I'm glad you enjoyed this foray into an alternative version of 1960s Hollywood.

To my agent, Stacia Decker, of the Dunow, Carlson &

Lerner Literary Agency—well, I don't even know where to begin. You are the best agent in the world, and a great friend. Thank you for everything you do. I'm so glad we're on this adventure together.

And finally, to my wife, Sandra. Through thick and thin, ups and downs, nights and weekends lost to the work, you are always there for me, and you have my back no matter what. I love you!

THE SPIDER WARS TRILOGY

ADAM CHRISTOPHER

THE BURNING DARK

Captain Abraham Idaho Cleveland has one last mission before early retirement: decommissioning a semi-deserted research outpost on the edge of Fleetspace. Isolated and paranoid, Ida reaches out to the universe via radio, only to tune into a disturbing signal. Is the transmission just a random burst of static from the past—or a warning of an undying menace that threatens humanity's future?

THE MACHINE AWAKES

In this far future space opera set in the Spider War universe of *The Burning Dark*, a government agent uncovers a conspiracy that stretches from the slums of Salt City to the floating gas mines of Jupiter. There, deep in the roiling clouds of the planet, the Jovian Mining Corporation is hiding a secret that will tear the Fleet apart. But there is something else hiding in Jovian system. Something insidious, intelligent and hungry. The Spiders are near.

THE DEAD STARS
AVAILABLE JANUARY 2019

When the test flight of the U-Star Manhattan—the first of a new class of starship—goes wrong, the seven-person crew find themselves shipwrecked, trapped in the interstitial nothingness that separates our universe from the next. But as the crew start to disappear one by one and the true purpose of their secret mission is uncovered, the survivors make a startling discovery about the eternal void they are lost in forever. They are not alone.

PRAISE FOR THE SERIES

"A creepy mystery embedded in a classic sci-fi setting that'll make you shiver…"
Tobias S. Buckell, *New York Times* bestselling author

"Christopher puts sci-fi in a metaphysical choke-hold—
The Burning Dark makes reality tap out."
Scott Sigler, *New York Times* bestselling author

"A riveting sci-fi mystery reminiscent of Shirley Jackson's
The Haunting of Hill House."
Martha Wells, author of
Star Wars: Empire and Rebellion—Razor's Edge

THE DIRE EARTH CYCLE

JASON M. HOUGH

The Builders came to Earth and constructed an elevator from Darwin, Australia into space. No one knows why, or if they will return.

Years later, a virus ravaged the planet. The rare immunes survived, others became something less than human. The elevator protected from the virus. The rich colonised the cord as the city below collapsed. But now the alien technology is failing. Will humanity survive?

THE DARWIN ELEVATOR
THE EXODUS TOWERS
THE PLAGUE FORGE
INJECTION BURN
ESCAPE VELOCITY

"Claustrophobic, intense, and satisfying. I couldn't put this book down. The Darwin Elevator depicts a terrifying world, suspends it from a delicate thread, and forces you to read with held breath as you anticipate the inevitable fall."
Hugh Howey, *New York Times* bestselling author of *Wool*

VICIOUS

V.E. SCHWAB

Victor and Eli started out as college roommates—brilliant, arrogant, lonely boys who recognized the same ambition in each other. A shared interest in adrenaline, near-death experiences, and seemingly supernatural events reveals an intriguing possibility: that under the right conditions, someone could develop extraordinary abilities. But when their thesis moves from the academic to the experimental, things go horribly wrong.

Ten years later, Victor breaks out of prison, determined to catch up to his old friend (now foe), aided by a young girl with a stunning ability. Meanwhile, Eli is on a mission to eradicate every other super-powered person that he can find—aside from his sidekick, an enigmatic woman with an unbreakable will. Armed with terrible power on both sides, driven by the memory of betrayal and loss, the arch-nemeses have set a course for revenge—but who will be left alive at the end?

"Supremely plotted and incredibly well-written."
The Independent on Sunday

TITANBOOKS.COM

KOKO TAKES A HOLIDAY

KIERAN SHEA

Five hundred years from now, ex-corporate mercenary Koko Martstellar is swaggering through an easy early retirement as a brothel owner on The Sixty Islands, a manufactured tropical resort archipelago known for its sex and simulated violence. Surrounded by slang-drooling boywhores and synthetic komodo dragons, Koko finds the most challenging part of her day might be deciding on her next drink.

That is, until her old comrade Portia Delacompte sends a squad of security personnel to murder her.

Now Koko is on the run in the sky-barges of the Second Free Zone—dodging ruthless eye-eating bounty agents dispatched by Delacompte and falling in with Flynn, a depressed local cop readying his nerves for a sanctioned mass suicide known as Embrace…

"Brutal, smart and wickedly funny."
Stephen Blackmore, author of *Dead Things*

TITANBOOKS.COM